WHEN THE MEN COME HOME

A NOVEL BY
JUDITH A. PERKINS

EXPLORA BOOKS
700 – 838 West Hastings St. Vancouver, BC V6C 0A6
www.explorabooks.com Phone:
(604) 330 6795

ISBN: 978-1-997587-12-5 (Paperback)
978-1-997587-13-2 (eBook)

WHEN THE MEN COME HOME

BY JUDITH PERKINS

An exploration of wartime sacrifice, the evolving role of women, post-war adjustment, and the enduring strength of *love and family*.

Table of Contents

Cast of Characters

Helen Cunningham	Protagonist
David Cunningham	Helen's husband joined the Navy – worked in Shipyards on Swan Island
Willard Martin	Helen's Father
Jane Martin	Helen's Mother
Roger Cunningham	David's father
Alice Cunningham	David's Mother
Daryl Oliver	Personal Mgr. Continental Can Co.
Richard Martin	Helen's Brother
Cheryl Martin	Richard's wife – Helen's sister-in-law
Jeremy Martin	Richard and Cheryl's son
Gloria Timms	Helen's oldest sister
Joshua (Josh) Timms	Gloria's husband
Laura Timms	Gloria and Josh's oldest daughter
Donna Timms	Gloria and Josh's youngest daughter
Marian Jamison	Helen's Sister
Michael Jamison	Helen's brother-in-law
Ellen & Ethel Jamison	Marian and Michael's twin daughters
Alex Smith	Continental Can Inventory Control Clerk {Helen replaced him}
Marvin Swenson	Helen's immediate boss
Greg Salazar	Head supervisor of all Inventory control employees.
Timothy Jacobs, MD	Alice Cunningham's Doctor
Capt. Ronald Walker	Doctor at Barnes Hospital, Vancouver, WA
Mrs. Bremer	Lady from the Methodist church
Rev. Mark Corbin	Pastor at Methodist Church
Edith Carpenter	Personnel Clerk at Sears
Mr. Keith Jacobs	Personnel Manager at Sears.
Stanley	The Dog!

Chapter 1

On December 7, 1941, the Japanese bombed Pearl Harbor in the Hawaiian Islands and the world changed. Life as people knew it no longer existed. Men went off to war and women were left without husbands, fathers, sons, brothers, and boyfriends.

Possibly of a greater concern, companies were left without workers. Because the United States was in the war now, it was vital that goods and services remain active and viable. Manufacturers were crying for workers and the only workers left to do the jobs were the women. It appalled some of the older men that they had to work alongside a woman, but the job had to be done and women were all that was left.

Helen Cunningham was one of those women. She was 22 years old, and married to David Cunningham, also 22 years old, for two years. They both went to college at Oregon State College in Corvallis, Oregon, but only made it through one year. David had done fairly well in school, but Helen was not a very attentive student and wanted to get on with her life. David couldn't afford to continue with school and had to work to pay for the tuition and room and board, so he quit at the same time Helen did.

David worked in the shipyards on Swan Island and Helen worked as a clerk in the handbag section of Sears Roebuck and Co. on Grand Avenue in Northeast Portland. They lived in a small apartment in North Portland about halfway between both of their jobs. David had an old car that he drove back and forth to the shipyards and Helen took the trolley to work every morning and home at night. They were supremely happy with their lives as they were and were even talking about maybe starting a family.

Both of their families lived in Portland and they spent their Sundays alternating between their parents' homes for dinner. Every week, one or the other of the mothers would ask if a baby was on the way, but the couple were very quiet about their feelings. Their standard answer to both mothers was, "Maybe someday."

On Sunday, December 7, 1941, David and Helen were about ready to leave her parents' home when the symphony music was interrupted on the radio with an urgent message that the Japanese had attacked the United States Fleet at Pearl Harbor in Hawaii.

David and Helen sat back down to listen to the broadcast in stunned silence at the announcement.

"Oh God, we are in it now!" bemoaned Willard Martin, Helen's father. "Roosevelt will send our boys to both Europe and Japan."

"You won't have to go, will you, David?" Helen asked pleadingly.

"Sure, I will, if they call me up," he answered.

"But David, you can't be called up. You are married. They wouldn't take married men, would they?" Helen asked.

"Helen, don't be so naïve!" her father said. "They are going to take anyone who is physically able to serve. Just because David is married doesn't mean he isn't able to serve."

"But Daddy, he already works at the shipyards. Shouldn't that be part of his contribution to the war?" Helen whined.

"It doesn't work that way, Helen. The Army and Navy need men to be battle ready. Working at the shipyards does not make a man battle ready," her father answered.

"I'm sure it will be several months until they have a plan for drafting men into the military. I think if I were to go in, I would choose the Navy. I have always liked the idea of sailing the Ocean Blue," David remarked.

"Well, we had better get home. I have to go to work early in the morning," Helen said. "Thanks for dinner, Mama."

"You two drive safely now. There are liable to be some wild drivers out tonight with the news on the radio. Call me when you get home," Jane said to her daughter.

"Okay, Mama!" Helen said as she walked out the door.

While they were driving home, Helen commented, "Maybe we should have a baby now. That would surely stop them from forcing you into the Army. Being a father should make you exempt from going away."

"Again, sweetheart, it doesn't work that way. As your Dad said, they need men who are battle ready, and just because I would have a child doesn't make me exempt from serving. Anyway, I kind of want to go into the Navy. Maybe I could kill some of the Japs who destroyed our ships," David commented.

"Don't say that, David. I do not want you to go into the service. You belong with me here at home. What will I do if you are gone?" Helen asked.

"You will continue working and do your part to help the war effort. The country is going to need all the help it can get, both men and women."

As expected, the next day, December 8th, all the news was about Roosevelt's speech to the Congress asking for a declaration of war. There were some people who were very upset about the declaration, but others were glad we were going to go to war.

The Christmas holiday was pretty subdued this year. David and Helen spent Christmas Eve with his parents, Roger and Alice Cunningham. On Christmas morning, they headed for

Helen's parents' home to spend the day with her brother, Richard, and sisters, Gloria and Marian, and their children. Helen knew it would be a madhouse with all of the kids around, and she wasn't really in the mood to celebrate. She didn't like the idea that David wanted to leave and join the Navy.

"Helen, I joined the Navy today," David announced as he walked into the house in January 1942. "I leave on Monday, the 12th, for San Diego for basic training. Then, I will probably be assigned to a ship and leave for the Pacific."

Helen was standing in front of the stove, stirring some soup for supper. She turned around and looked at David in stunned silence.

"What did you say?" Helen asked in amazement.

"I said I joined the Navy today," David repeated.

Helen looked at David like she didn't understand what he had said. She was stunned that he would enlist without talking to her first.

"Why did you do a stupid thing like that? I told you I didn't want you to leave. If we had a baby now, you wouldn't have to go. You would be a father," Helen yelled at him. "That was really dumb. Tomorrow morning, you go back to where you enlisted and tell them you made a mistake."

"I can't do that, Helen. I already signed the paper and it is binding. I cannot get out of it unless I don't pass the physical, and there is very little chance that I won't pass. I work in the shipyards and have to pass their physicals every year, which I do," David explained. "If I wait to be drafted, they will put me in the Army, in the infantry probably, and I would be miserable. I want to be in the Navy. They get better food and at least have a bunk to sleep in onboard the ship. In the Army, I would have to sleep on the ground or in a foxhole. That's not for me!"

"When do you have to leave and where do you go?" Helen asked very quietly.

"I leave for San Diego in two weeks. That gives me time to wrap things up at the shipyards and get all of my papers in order here. I think it would be a good idea if we give up this apartment and you move back in with your parents for a while. We don't need the extra expense of the apartment while I am gone, and I am sure your parents would love to have you back living with them," David said.

"No! I will not move back into my parents' home. They would take control of my life again and I will not live like that again. Daddy would question everything that I do and treat me like a teenager. I will not be under his thumb," Helen stated firmly. "I will find a cheaper apartment or will get one of my girlfriends at work to move in and share the rent."

They ate their dinner in silence. Helen got up and cleaned up the kitchen while David went in to listen to the news on the radio.

It was reported that over three thousand people were killed in Hawaii, both military and civilians. The most casualties were on the USS Arizona when a Japanese bomb made a direct hit on the ship, causing a horrendous fire and mass casualties.

Helen went in to sit beside David, but couldn't stand all of the doom and gloom coming from the radio, so she went to bed instead.

Chapter 2

David was busy during the two weeks before he had to leave for San Diego and basic training. He made sure that Helen was listed on his bank account and that a life insurance policy that he had purchased when he graduated from high school had listed her as the beneficiary. He also transferred the title to his car over to her. He wanted to make sure that, if anything did happen to him, she would have access to all of his necessary documents.

Helen thought that David was being incredibly kind to think of her well-being. What she didn't know was that he was working off of a list given to him by the recruiter. It was a list of things that should be done before he leaves. The military services felt that it was better if the men themselves took care of all of this instead of leaving it up to a loved one in case of their death.

Two days before David was to leave, the recruiter called him to tell him he was taking a train instead of a bus to San Diego. David was relieved to hear that. The idea of sitting up in a bus for three days was not a pleasant thought to him. At least in a train he would be able to put his seat back and he wouldn't have to get off of the train to eat his meal.

At 6:00 AM on January 12, David and Helen, David's parents and Helen's parents were at the Union Station in Portland to see David off to San Diego. Helen had been up almost the entire night before in tears at the thought that her husband would be away for such a long time. She did not want to move back into her parents' home, but could not as yet find a roommate that would be willing to share the rent with her, and she did not want a stranger in her home, so was limited to friends and co-workers. She had enough money saved to pay two months' rent, but after that, she had to have someone else pay half. David's Navy pay would not be enough to cover rent and utilities.

David's parents were stoic at the sight of him climbing onto the train. Helen thought that his mother would be in tears, but she was just standing there with a grim look on her face. She gave him a brief hug, but that was all. His father shook his hand and gave him a slap on the back saying, "Give 'em Hell, son."

Helen was trying so hard to be brave, but she was openly sobbing and clinging to David. As the time shortened before he had to board, David was also clinging to her.

"I love you sweetheart, and I will write to you as often as I can," he whispered to her. "You take good care of yourself. This war cannot last long and I will be home before you know it."

"David, what am I going to do without you?" Helen cried. "I miss you already."

"You will be fine," he answered. "You are strong and you will be okay."

David boarded the train with all of the other recruits. He stood at the open window by his seat and waved to his family for as long as he could before he had to close the window and sit down.

Helen walked with her family back to the parking lot to the car. Her mother did not want her to drive in the state she was in, but Helen insisted that she would drive herself home. She was going to go to work in the afternoon and wanted to get into her work clothes and get something to eat before she left for work.

Helen reported for work in the handbag department of Sears at 12:00 O'clock noon with red puffy eyes. She had said nothing about David leaving to any of her co-workers, so they were concerned about the late arrival and about her red eyes.

"I needed the morning off because my husband left for basic training in San Diego this morning."

"Why didn't you tell us before that he was leaving? We would have covered the entire day for you instead of just the morning," one of the other ladies asked.

"To tell you the truth, I didn't want to think about it. I didn't really believe until this morning that he would leave," Helen answered.

"Is that why you were asking about a roommate?" someone else asked.

"Yes. David's Navy pay will not cover half of the rent and utilities. I am going to have to find a smaller, cheaper place to stay or move back in with my folks. I really don't want to do that. David and I have been on our own for two years and I don't want to be back under my father's thumb. I know that he would treat me like a teenager again," Helen explained.

Business was pretty slow at work that day and Helen was glad when 5:30 came along and she could go home. The thought of going home to an empty house was not pleasing to her, but she didn't want to go to her parents or her in-laws for supper. They had both invited her saying that they didn't think it was a good idea for her to be alone that evening, but she insisted that she would be okay, that she had some things that she needed to do that evening.

Helen stopped at the newsstand on the way home to buy a newspaper. She picked up both the Oregonian and the Journal wanting to keep up with all of the war news. Because David was in the Navy, she wanted to be sure she knew what was going on in the world.

When she got home, she started to cry when she went into the apartment and David wasn't there. He usually was home before she was. She could smell him when she went into their bedroom to change her clothes. She opened their closet and buried her face in his clothes. Finally, she pulled herself together, changed her clothes, and went into the kitchen to get some supper. After putting a pan of leftovers into the oven to heat, she sat down with the papers and started to read them.

As she ate her meal, she noticed an ad on one of the back pages of the Oregonian for workers at the shipyards. They were advertising for women to come in to apply for jobs. Because all of the men were joining the military services, the shipyards were clamoring for workers. They still had to continue building ships. The need for them was greater now than ever before. With the fleet damaged so badly at Pearl Harbor, the ships had to be replaced. The yards at Swan Island were not building the huge battleships, but they were building some of the smaller support ships and they badly needed workers to fill the positions left empty by the men who had left.

Helen read the advertisement twice. She was intrigued by the idea of working in a business where the employees were predominantly men and the salary, she would receive was over double what she was making now. She might still need a roommate to make ends meet, but her chances of finding someone would be a lot better at the shipyard than at Sears. Handbags would not be a priority now. Ships and related military equipment would be the priority for the time being.

Helen noticed that the same advertisement was in the Oregon Journal newspaper as well. She also read an advertisement for the Continental Can Company needing employees in their plant making tin cans for eventual packing of food rations for the troops in both Europe and in the Pacific. She was very interested in that ad because Continental Can was only about a mile and a half from her apartment and she would be able to walk to work when the weather was good. The shipyards were a good 30-minute bus ride away.

She decided to go to the employment office at Continental Can on her next day off and apply for a job. The advertisement did not give the salary, but Helen was sure it would be more than she was making now.

Her next day off was Tuesday and she took the bus to the employment office. The office was in a separate building from the actual manufacturing plant.

There was a line of women waiting for applications, so Helen had to wait. She took the application when it was her turn in line and went to a desk to fill it out.

After reviewing Helen's application, the receptionist asked her to please have a seat and wait. There would be someone out to speak to her very soon. The receptionist took Helen's application into another office and came out to ask Helen to follow her. There she met Daryl Oliver, the personnel manager at Continental Can.

"Have a seat Mrs. Cunningham. Trudy brought me your application because she noticed you work in retail. What do you do in retail?" Mr. Oliver asked.

"I sell handbags at Sears Roebuck and Company," Helen answered.

"How long have you worked there and what are some of your duties, besides selling?" Mr. Oliver asked again.

"Well, I keep track of the inventory. If we are getting low on the inventory of a particular handbag, I report it to my manager and she reorders if the budget permits and if it is a popular item. The manager is over three different departments in the store, handbags, millinery, and shoes, so he doesn't have a lot of time to oversee specific inventory in each department. He relies on the employees to do that for him," Helen explained.

"I see you have had some college. Did you quit for financial reasons?" the manager asked.

"Partly, but I met my husband there and I really wasn't a very good student and didn't really like college. Both of us quit so that we could get married. He went to work at the shipyards and I went to work at Sears," Helen continued. "We got along very well on our two salaries, but now with David in the Navy, I just can't make it on my salary alone and the Navy pay doesn't make up the difference."

"Well, Mrs. Cunningham, Continental Can is looking for someone to work in the inventory control division of the plant. Inventory control keeps track of the number of cans in each size and shape that we make. Different foods are packed into different size cans. It is paramount that we have the proper size cans available to ship to the areas where they are filled and then sent overseas for use. Part of your responsibilities would be to let the production managers know what is needed and when it is needed. We cannot afford to have any downtime, so it is imperative that the plant runs like a clock at all times. Each size can has its own production line and part of your duties would be to let them know when they have to speed up production or when they can dial back a bit. We do not have a lot of storage space. As soon as the cans are ready, they are shipped to the plant in Northwest Portland and packed for shipment overseas," Mr. Oliver continued to explain to her. "Would you be interested in a position like that? It carries a great deal of responsibility to it. There would, of course, be a training period. We do not throw our employees into the deep end right away."

"You did not post what the salary would be," Helen stated. "I would have to make quite a bit more than I am right now to be able to make ends meet."

"Your beginning wage would be $20.00 per week with an increase to $25.00 per week after a four-week training period. This salary is a little higher than a lot of the women working here now because you have some inventory control experience," Mr. Oliver explained.

"That is a very generous salary and is much more than I am making now. That and David's pay would cover my rent and utilities without the need for a roommate," Helen commented. "I would be more than happy to accept the job. When would you want me to start?"

"As soon as possible. With all of the men going off to war, we are in dire need of help," Mr. Oliver explained.

"I would feel much better giving Sears at least a week's notice. Would Monday, January 26th be okay to start?" she asked.

"That would be fine. We would like it to be sooner, but I understand your wanting to give your current employer some notice. I have some papers for you to fill out before you start work. Would you like to do it now?" Mr. Oliver asked.

"That would be fine. I have the time now," Helen answered.

Chapter 3

Helen took the bus home after she finished filling out all of the paperwork that Mr. Oliver gave her. She was excited about the new job and doubly excited about the increase in salary that she would have. Her father would not like the fact that she was not going to move home and that she would be working in a predominately male occupation, but at this point, she did not care. She was determined not to be under her father's thumb again.

On Wednesday, Helen went to the personnel office at Sears and turned in her resignation. Her last day of work would be Saturday, January 26th. The personnel department was not surprised at Helen's resignation. They had had a rash of them in the last few days. Many of their women employees were leaving to replace the men in the factories and manufacturing plants in the Portland area.

The store certainly understood the situation and sympathized with the women. They had a feeling that for a while customers would be few and far between. There would be no new appliances being manufactured. All of the metal was being diverted to ships or airplanes. Ammunition was of the highest priority now. Leather for handbags and shoes would be diverted to the making of uniforms and leather boots and straps for guns. New handbags were going to be a luxury for the duration of the war.

The telephone was ringing as Helen walked into her apartment after work. When she picked it up, her father was on the line.

"Come to dinner tomorrow. I want to discuss your living arrangements," he ordered.

"I will come to dinner, Dad, but I will not alter my living arrangements. I am staying here in David's and my home," Helen firmly stated.

"We'll see! Come tomorrow about 1:00 PM," her father ordered again.

"You will see me when I get there. Have a good evening, Father," Helen answered as she hung up the phone.

Dinner at her parents' home was not going to be very pleasant tomorrow. She didn't know whether her brother and sisters would be there or not. She kind of wished she was going to David's parents' home instead, but she hadn't been invited since he left.

Helen dialed her in-law's phone number and her mother-in-law answered. "Hello Alice, this is Helen. How are you?" she asked.

"I know who you are and how do you think I am? My son has left for the war and might never come back," Alice Cunningham moaned.

"Please don't say that, Alice. David will come home. I know it!" Helen insisted.

"Well, I don't!" she stated firmly. "What did you call for?"

"I just wanted to say 'hello' and ask how you were doing," Helen said.

"Well, I'm busy now and don't have time for your chit-chat. Call when you have something to say that is important," Alice said as she hung up the phone.

Helen sat there in stunned silence. What did she do? She didn't do anything to Alice Cunningham, except marry her precious son. Alice had never forgiven her for marrying her precious son, like it was all Helen's fault. David is the one who asked her and the one who wanted to get married right away. It was probably to get away from his mother, Helen thought.

Helen arrived at her parent's home at 2:10 in the afternoon. Her sisters and brother were there with all of their kids and the place looked like a tornado had hit it. There were toys all over the place. Her sister and mother were in the kitchen putting the finishing touches on the dinner, and her father, brother, and brothers-in-law were sitting around listening to the war news. No one was supervising the children and they were running around the house like wild Indians.

Helen tried to corral them and sit them down with some books, but they would have none of it. She finally gave up and walked into the living room. There were already too many people in the kitchen and they didn't need her help.

Willard Martin stood up and insisted that Helen sit in his seat. She was suspicious about his motives, but sat anyway. He stood at the fireplace like the lord of the manor and started talking.

"Helen, your brother and brothers-in-law and I have been discussing your situation and this is what we have come up with. You will move back home with your mother and me, and you will take care of your nieces and nephews while the girls go work at the shipyards. There are jobs available for them right away, but they cannot work without child care. The boys will be going into the Army soon and the girls will need the jobs to supplement their pay. The boys will all help you move, and you can be settled back in your old room by Monday," Helen's father pronounced as if it was a done deal.

"No!" said Helen.

"What did you say?" asked her father.

"I said No! I will not move back here and I will not babysit those children. It is not my job to teach them manners. It is their parents' and obviously by the looks of things, they are not doing a very good job of it. Daddy, I will not live under your thumb again. I have a new job starting Monday the 26th. I will be working in the inventory control office at Continental Can Company. I will be making a decent salary and will be able to keep my apartment without getting a roommate," Helen stated firmly.

"You what?" Willard Martin roared. "You will march back to that employment office and tell them that you are not taking that job and you will do as I tell you to."

Helen spoke in a calm voice. "I will do nothing of the sort, Father. I am 23 years old, have been married for two years, and have been living with my husband for those two years. I will not go back to being a child, and there is really nothing you can do about it. I'm sorry, but my mind is made up. I will go into the kitchen and say goodbye to the ladies. Obviously, my presence is not wanted here right now," Helen said as she got up from the chair and went towards the kitchen.

"You stop!" yelled Willard.

Helen kept walking into the kitchen. She said goodbye to Gloria and Marian and her mother and started to leave via the back door. Her sisters stopped her and pleaded with her to take care of their children so they could go out and work, but again she said no and explained why she wouldn't.

"Take a look around this house. There are toys, clothes, food, and trash strewn everywhere. Your children have no manners or discipline. It is not my job to do that. It is yours, and until you take your responsibilities seriously, I will have none of it. I love my nieces and nephew, but I will not be their parent. And I will not move back into this house and be under our father's thumb again. Anyway, I have a new job and I start on Monday, so I am not available," she said as she walked out the back door.

Helen got into her car and started the engine. Just then her mother came running out of the house calling for her to stop. She pleaded with Helen to come back in and talk about the situation. She would be so much safer living there with her family.

"No, Mother! I cannot go through all that garbage with Dad another time. It was bad enough the first time around. Never again. I will see you some other time when Dad isn't around," Helen explained, and then she drove away from the curb, leaving her mother standing there in tears.

On Monday, the 26th of January 1942, Helen Cunningham started working for Continental Can Company in North Portland. She loved her job from the very beginning and proved to be very good at it. She had always been good with numbers and was meticulous in keeping the inventory records. Her fellow employees loved her. She made good friends with several of the ladies working in the office and even some of them who worked on the manufacturing floor. Helen found it fascinating watching the process of pressing the metal and cutting it to fit the requirements for the specific size cans. She did not realize that meat had its own size can, as did vegetables, potatoes, fruit, pudding, etc. The GIs could tell pretty much what they had to eat by the size of the can they were opening. Of course, they were all labeled also, but that was done at the packing plant after they were filled.

It did not take long for Helen to learn the ins and outs of her job and some of the other employees started coming to her for answers to their questions. She was very careful not to answer them without checking with either her supervisor or theirs.

Helen had had several letters from David. He was concerned about the rift between her and her family. He thought that she should move home and give up their apartment, but again, she refused and gave him the same reasoning that she did her dad, mom, and sisters.

The biggest blow to Helen was when David wrote and said he would not be coming home before he was shipped out to Hawaii. He was assigned to a troop carrier going right from San Diego to Pearl Harbor. From there he would probably be assigned to a cargo ship delivering supplies to other ships at sea.

"I would like to be assigned to a battleship or destroyer, cruiser, or some ship that would actually fight the Japanese, but this is what I am assigned to now. When I have a little time underneath my belt, I will probably ask for a transfer," David wrote to his wife. "San Diego is a really pretty city. The weather is fantastic. It has been warm and sunny most of the time, not like Portland at all. I wish you could see it, but we can't afford to have you come here. There would be nothing for you to do all day while I am at work and I will be leaving soon anyway."

Helen had written David telling him about her new job, but she hadn't heard back from him yet. She also wrote him about his mother's attitude towards her. She probably wouldn't have much contact with her until David got back. She also wrote to him about her father and his demands of her. She also told him about her sisters and how they were mad at her for not staying home and taking care of their children. She relayed to David her exact words to them also. He would get a big laugh out of that.

She knew that once he was at sea, the mail would come at a snail's pace. It could be weeks before she heard from him. She wasn't very happy about his being out of touch for so long, but there was nothing she could do about it. She was going to enjoy her job at the plant and make some new friends. Her high school friends were long gone and she had not made any really good friends at Sears and she was ready for some female companionship.

Chapter 4

Even though Helen missed David terribly, life was good for her right now. She was enjoying her job, taking on new responsibilities all of the time and making new friends. Some of her friends went out in the evenings for drinks, but she hadn't done that with them yet. Helen was not much of a drinker, and she was not interested in prowling around bars looking for men. She already had one and wasn't tempted by others. She tried to explain that to her friends, but they didn't understand. The one thing that her father had instilled in her was loyalty, and she was completely loyal and faithful to David.

Helen had very little contact with David's family. His mother was uncommunicative about almost everything, and she was never invited to their home anymore. While David was home, there didn't seem to be any problems between them, but the minute he was gone, a barrier came up, and she couldn't seem to penetrate it. She didn't want to bother David with her problems, so she didn't write to him about it. He did mention in one of his letters that his mother said that Helen didn't contact her anymore. He wanted to know why, but she was hesitant in telling him. He had enough on his mind battling the Japanese without mediating battles between his wife and his parents.

She also avoided going to her parents' home. Occasionally, she would make an appearance, but never stayed long. Her father would start in on her, and she would leave. And her nieces and nephews were so loud and messy that she couldn't stand to be around them. They had no respect for anyone else's property. At one point when she was over at her parents' house, she caught her nephew going through her purse. When questioned about it, he said it was just sitting there, and he was curious.

She told her sister, Gloria, to keep her kids away from her property, and her sister was all bent out of shape about the comment. Her comment was, "Well, he is just a curious child."

"He can be a curious child about other people's property if that is the way you are raising him, but keep him away from mine. And, never bring your children to my home. They are not welcome there if their manners do not improve a lot," Helen commented. "I am surprised at you for raising your children that way. One of the good things Dad did for all of us is teach us to be honest and loyal to family and friends. That is the one lesson I learned, and I try to live by."

"Well, you can follow the old way of raising children. My children are going to be free and be able to do what they want to in life," Gloria snorted at Helen.

"Well, I hope you don't have to visit them in jail someday. At the rate they are going at such a young age, you just might be doing that," Helen said as she left the house by the back door.

Helen's father had heard her comment about his lessons on trust, loyalty, and integrity. For the first time in a long time, he was very proud of his youngest daughter. He hadn't thought about those talks that he and Helen had when she was young for a long time. He was very glad that the lessons had sunk in. And he was pretty embarrassed to be out and about with his grandchildren in tow. They were rude and abusive to other children and to adults around them. Maybe he would have to sit them down and have some serious talks with them.

Helen was upset again when she got home from her parents' home. It was not worth it to go over there, but she missed her family. She wasn't sure whether she actually missed her family or missed the idea of a family.

When she walked in the door, the phone was ringing, and she had to run for it. It was her father on the line.

"Hello Dad. I just left your house. Did I forget something?" she asked.

"No, but I did! Can I come over to your place for a few minutes? I need to talk to you about something," Willard Martin asked.

"Yes, but don't bother if you are going to try to change my mind on moving into your house with you and Mom," she stated firmly. "I will not listen to any more of that talk."

"No, it's not that. It's something else entirely," Willard said.

"Okay, I will see you in a bit," Helen said as she hung up, wondering what that was all about.

She hung up her coat and put a pot of coffee on. She knew her dad liked his cup of coffee in the evening. While the coffee was brewing, she straightened up a bit, washed some dishes left in the sink that morning, and put them in the dish drainer. She made sure that any important papers were put away so that her father would not see them. She did not want him involved in any of her business, especially financial. She was making good money at Continental Can and was able to put David's Navy pay into a savings account at the bank. As long as she didn't need to use it for anything, she would save as much as she could for him to use when he got home. The one thing she wanted to do is keep his car in good running condition so that he would have transportation when he returned.

Her father pulled his car up to the front of her apartment about an hour after he called. He had a slight smile on his face when he walked into her apartment and gave her a brief hug, which was something he rarely ever did. He was not a physically affectionate person, and it surprised her when he hugged her.

"Have a seat, Dad. I made some coffee for you. I know you like your evening cup of coffee," Helen said. She went into the kitchen to get the coffee and sugar bowl and brought it out to the coffee table.

"This is a really nice apartment. You and David really lucked out when you got this one," her dad said, trying to make small talk. He wasn't sure how to get started with what he wanted to say to her.

"What is it you wanted to talk about, Dad?" Helen asked.

"I really don't know where to start. I want you to know that I heard what you said to your sister the other day about the lessons I taught you about honesty, loyalty, and integrity. I didn't mean to eavesdrop. I was coming into the kitchen and overheard what you were saying. I didn't know you were listening to me when you were younger. You always seemed to be bored with what I said. I really didn't know if anything I ever said made any impact on you at all. I guess something did," Willard said. "I am truly sorry for treating you so badly. You are my youngest child, my little girl, and I want everything to be perfect for you. I am afraid for you to live here alone. I still want to protect you. Now with David gone, I am doubly afraid, but I have to realize that you are an adult and are capable of making your own decisions. I didn't realize that until tonight when I heard you talking to your sisters and your mother. I looked around the house and saw the mess those kids have made of my home and heard the disrespect coming from their mouths and your sister's mouths. At that point, I realized that you were the only adult in the group, and you, of all my children, deserved my respect and admiration more than the others right now," Willard Martin continued. "Helen, I love all of my children, but right now you are holding a special place in my heart for standing up for what you believe in and standing up to your bully of a father. You have made a beautiful home here for you and David. After seeing this and then looking at my house and the condition it is in with those kids around, no wonder you do not want to move back in. You would be moving away from your home, not back to it."

Helen was astounded at what her father had said. That was about the longest she had heard him talk without giving an order in a very long time.

"Thank you, Dad. I really don't know what to say right now. I would not survive in the confusion of your house for very long. A Sunday afternoon meal is about all I can handle. And the idea of me staying home and taking care of those kids while their mothers go out and work is ridiculous. Like I told them, it is not my responsibility to raise them. It is theirs," Helen stated. "When you were talking about honesty when we were little, I didn't think about being honest with others, but being honest with myself as well, and I have you to thank for that."

Helen got up from her chair, walked over to her dad, and bent down and gave him a hug.

When Willard Martin left his daughter's later that evening, he was walking with a lighter step and making some decisions about what to do about his other daughters and their children. Right now, the children pretty much had the run of the house. That was going to stop.

Jane Martin was alone in the house when Willard returned. The living room floor was still strewn with toys, dirty dishes, and pillows and blankets. It looked like the grandkids had made a fort, with the upturned dining room chairs, but left without picking things up. Jane was just too tired to clean it all up right now.

"I will get to this in a moment, Willard," Jane said. "Let me rest for a moment."

"You rest. I will clean this up," Willard remarked as if it was a usual thing for him to help clean. Jane was stunned when he started folding the blankets and putting the pillows back on the sofa and chairs where they belonged. He righted the chairs and put them back up to the dining table, then started taking the dirty dishes into the kitchen, placed them in the sink, and ran hot water over them.

All the time he was doing this, Jane was sitting in her chair with her mouth agape, unable to speak. She couldn't remember the last time he had helped her clean up.

"Jane, some changes are going to be made around here. I had my eyes opened to the chaos in this house when the grandchildren are here. Helen made some comments that rang true, and we are partially at fault for allowing the grandkids to treat us the way they do. And, we are at fault for allowing our girls to do the same thing. They are not giving their children any boundaries or any sense of value at all," Willard said to his wife. "I do not want to do it because I love my children and grandchildren, but I do not want them in this house until they can show some respect for us and our property and show that they have some manners when they are with their elders."

"Oh, Willard, thank you. I didn't say anything because I was afraid that you would disagree, but the mess and destruction of property is more than I can take sometimes. I have tried to quietly say something to the girls, but they do not respond favorably. They say they want their children to have the freedom to express themselves the way they want to," Jane commented.

"Unfortunately, with that attitude, as Helen said, they will be visiting their children in jail if they don't change their ways now. I will talk to them. Around here, things will change or they will not be invited over here," Willard stated with authority.

Chapter 5

Life took on a routine for Helen. She would get up in the morning, shower, put her work clothes on, and have a cup of coffee and a piece of toast before she left for the bus stop to go to work. Continental Can Co. was running three shifts a day, and Helen was fortunate enough to be permanently on the day shift.

When the work day was over, Helen would reverse the process and head for home on the bus. Sometimes, when the weather was decent, she would walk home. There were several shops along the way, and she always enjoyed the walk when the window displays had been changed. Summer clothes had been in the dress shop window for two months now. Of course, she couldn't afford to buy anything new. She was doing okay financially with her pay and David's Navy pay to supplement if necessary. She was trying to bank all of his pay, though, so they would have a nest egg when he returned.

She would receive a letter here and there, but they all seemed to be disjointed, and she never knew where he was. All she knew was that he was on a supply ship that would transfer supplies to other ships in the middle of the ocean, but he never said anything about what he did on the ship or where they were or what ships they were supplying. She thought from reading the letters that some of them were missing. He dated them, but she never received them in chronological order. She would write to David every evening but would mail the letters once a week. She was never sure if he received them or not. He never mentioned anything about what she had written.

Helen had an ache in her heart all of the time and missed David most of all in the evening when they would lie in bed and talk to each other about their dreams for the future. Every night now, she would pray that they had a future and that he would come home safe.

The months went by with no positive word about the war. Hitler and the Nazi party were still marching through Europe, raising havoc on the allied military force there and on the civilians in every country. The Pacific seemed to be a hotbed of fighting. Lt. Colonel James Doolittle made a daring raid on Tokyo, the first raid on the Japanese Islands. The damage was not extensive, but the morale boost to the American troops and citizens was terrific. The battle of Midway Island in June of 1942 was a victory for the Americans and again boosted the morale of the people. It was reported that the American dive bombers sunk four Japanese aircraft carriers. Everyone at home was looking forward to that being the turning point of the war in the Pacific.

Helen wondered if David was involved in that battle. She had not heard from him in several weeks. The mail was very slow in getting to her, and she was constantly worried.

Her job in the inventory control department at Continental Can continued to be challenging for her. During the day while she was working, her mind was 100 percent on her work. She felt strongly that the lives of the soldiers and sailors depended on how well she managed the inventory of the food ration cans. If there was not enough, some soldier or sailor would not get a meal. If there were too many cans of one size being produced, it was a waste. She took her job seriously.

Occasionally, Helen would go out with some of the other girls in the plant. Most of the time, she chose the girls who had husbands overseas like she did. But she was never comfortable when strange men came up to her, so she never stayed long. She either spent her time at home or with her parents.

Helen's father had laid down the law to her sisters and brother about the lack of respect coming from their children and banned them from his house until they could behave. Both Gloria and Marian were not speaking to Helen at all now. They both felt that she was the cause of their father's new attitude towards his grandchildren. They always thought that Helen got what she wanted because she was the baby of the family.

Helen had no contact with her in-laws at all. She tried to call and talk to them, but they would not respond to her calls. When they heard her voice, they just hung up the phone. Finally, she quit calling.

The months went by, and before Helen knew it, David had been gone for a whole year. She had received a few letters from him, but none recently, and nothing indicated in the letters she did receive where he was. She did not even know what ship he was on.

She devoured the newspapers every day to see if she could try to figure out where he could be, but there were too many battles going on at a time to make any sense of it.

In the meantime, Helen did her job with great efficiency and enjoyed what she was doing. Her immediate supervisor promoted her several times and continually gave her increased responsibility. She had proved to all of them that she could do good work. The factory was always right on schedule for the number of cans that they had to produce in a certain amount of time.

Helen had a friend at the plant, Mary Neilson, whose husband was also in the Navy stationed in the Pacific somewhere. Mary got very few letters from her husband also, and she and Helen were worried about their husbands or even if they still had husbands.

The news was not good from a small island called Guadalcanal. Helen and Mary could barely pronounce the name. The fighting there had been going on for many months, and there was still no word of a victory for the Americans. Everyone was in need of some positive news for a change.

The news from Europe wasn't much better. Helen's brother Dick and one of her brothers-in-law were in Europe. They were both in the Army and were with the troops during the invasion of North Africa. Everyone was worried about them. Again, the mail was sporadic, and the family heard very little. Everyone devoured the news on the radio and in the newspapers.

Willard Martin had offered to take all four of his grandchildren on a camping trip for a weekend. He wanted to try and instill some honesty and integrity in them and thought that if he had their rapt attention, he would be able to talk to them and they would listen. All they were to bring were sleeping bags, extra clothes, and their pillows. There were no toys or games, and everything they brought was going to be shared with the others. Willard had one large tent, and they were going to all sleep together. They would cook their food over an open fire and would have to share what they had.

Helen had given her dad some of her gas ration cards. Because she rode the bus or walked to work, she did not use them as fast. He drove the kids along the Columbia River towards Astoria, to a small campground along the river near a town called St. Helens. The kids were excited about going with their grandpa. They missed going to their grandparents' house on Sundays for dinner. The thought of being free to do what they wanted for a weekend was exciting for them.

Little did they know what was in store for them!

"Okay kids, you are going to have an adventure this weekend, and maybe you will learn something too, but you have to listen to what I say very carefully. If you do not listen, you could be in trouble out here in the woods. I certainly do not want any one of you in trouble," Willard explained to the children. "You must stay together. If any one of you goes off on your own, you could be in serious trouble. There might be wild animals out here, and I don't want any of you eaten by a wild animal."

All four of the children were wide-eyed at the mention of wild animals. "We are all going to sleep in the tent together, so there will be no leaving your things out where other people could trip over them or worse yet, damage them. They are your private possessions, and you must be responsible for taking care of them."

"Grandpa, who is going to fix our dinner?" Jeremy asked.

"You are!" Willard explained. "Each one of you is going to be responsible for your own meals. If you do not fix your own meals, there will be no one else to do it for you. You will be in charge of your own meals. We have limited supplies, so we will have to share. That means, if we have five eggs available for breakfast, we will all get one egg. If one person is selfish and eats two eggs, someone else goes without."

"But Grandpa, we do not know how to cook," exclaimed Laura.

"You will either learn to cook your meals or you will go hungry. No one else is going to do it for you."

"Grandpa, I am a boy. I don't cook for myself. The women do that for us boys," Jeremy stated with conviction.

"Then Jeremy, my boy, you are in a lot of trouble. The girls are not going to cook for you, and neither am I. I will teach all of you to fix your own meals with what we have on hand. I brought enough food for all of us if we supplement with what we find in the wild. We are also going to try to catch some fish to cook. We are going to have some fun as well as you learning something about responsibility and generosity."

"Another thing, if I find your stuff strewn around this campsite and not put away where it belongs, it is going into the fire. If any of the food is left out where animals could get it and no one confesses to leaving it out, everyone goes hungry at the next scheduled meal. That includes me, and I do not like to go hungry, so please pick up after yourself," Willard emphasized.

The weekend was eye-opening for everyone, even Grandpa Willard. First of all, he was astounded at what the children did not know how to do. He didn't realize that they did not adhere to a specific meal time. Their parents let them eat whenever they felt like it, which made for a mess most of the time. Willard was also astounded to see them take direction and how much they seemed to want to learn. They were eager to follow the rules, especially since all of them had missed a meal because they did not pick up after themselves and keep the campground neat.

When the weekend camping trip was over and Willard had driven the children back to his house where their parents were picking them up, the children were exhausted but very happy, and one and all told Grandpa that they had a wonderful time and wanted to go camping with him again.

"Thanks, Grandpa, for showing me that I could do things for myself without having to wait for someone else to do them for me. I really liked being responsible for myself. I had a really good time and would like to go camping with you again sometime," Jeremy said to his Grandpa. Jeremy's mother heard what he had said and was astounded at his attitude. Usually, Jeremy had to be pushed and prodded to say something nice about anyone. She had never heard him so polite.

The children's mothers were surprised when the children came in, greeted everyone with respect, put their own camping gear away in Grandpa's garage where it belonged, and sat down on the sofa and chairs without jumping on them.

"What in the world did you do to these children, Willard?" Gloria asked. "I've never seen them this way."

"We had a wonderful weekend learning how to be polite and respectful to each other and to ourselves. We learned about having some self-control and learned how to take responsibility for our own actions. A couple of meals we all went hungry, but we made up for it in the fish we caught and cooked. By the way, Gloria, ask Jeremy to cook you some trout over an open fire sometime. It was very tasty. We all ate our fill of trout that night. Everyone caught one," Willard explained.

"We would love to have you all come for supper next Sunday. The kids have promised to help set the table and clean up afterward. I am going to ask Helen to come also. Maybe you can make up for differences now."

Everyone left about the same time, the grandchildren all giving their Grandpa a big hug and thank you and kissing and hugging their Grandma also.

There was much discussion in the cars on the way home about the camping weekend with Grandpa. The kids were very polite and explained what they did, but did not talk about what Grandpa had said during the weekend. They all wanted to be very polite and respectful to their grandfather.

Chapter 6

————◆ ◆ ◆ ————

1942 was drawing to a close with no sight of the war coming to an end and no hope for David coming home soon. All Helen knew was that he was on a troop carrier somewhere in the South Pacific.

The headlines for 1942 were very scary for the ones who cared about the sailors and marines: Midway, Bataan, Guadalcanal, Guam, The Philippines. They were all becoming familiar names now, when reading the newspaper. Helen was never sure what to expect when she listened to the news or read a newspaper. She had a large map of the Pacific theater of war posted on her bedroom wall. She was able to visualize the vast amount of water between each of the battle sites, but never knew where David was in all that space.

In November 1942, Helen received a packet of 17 letters that David had written to her. These were the first letters she had received in months. She cried when she picked up her mail and saw the letters. David had numbered them, so she was able to read them in order.

He was stationed aboard the USS Alden, a Clemson-class destroyer. He still couldn't say where he was or had been, but at least she knew he was still alive. She devoured the letters, which mostly told about life on board the ship and some funny anecdotes about some of his shipmates.

"Oh, my darling, how I wish you were here with me. I hate to admit it, but sometimes I forget what you looked like. I miss you so terribly," Helen said to herself when she had finished reading the stack of letters. She lovingly placed the letters in the top drawer of her dresser with the rest of the letters she had received from him, then called her father to let him know that she had heard from David.

Willard was excited that they finally knew what ship David was assigned to. If he was on a destroyer, that meant he was in the thick of the fighting, and he could be anywhere in the vast Pacific Ocean.

Helen tried to call David's parents, but they again hung up when they heard her voice. Helen was still stung by their attitude towards her. They were never that way before David left. She didn't remember doing or saying anything that would make them so antagonistic towards her. She was keeping track of the times that she called them, though. She didn't want them to tell David that she never tried to reach out to them. She kept a list of the times and dates of her calls right beside her phone.

Helen's life was pretty routine as 1943 approached. There were some good snippets of news coming from the war in Europe. The Allies had defeated the Germans in North Africa in November of 1942. Morale was lifted with that news, but the news in the Pacific was not as good. The campaign in Guadalcanal went back and forth. The Americans would have a victory, then the Japanese would send in fresh troops and take the territory back. The battle went on and on and back and forth, and too many Americans were dying. The casualty numbers were staggering.

Helen would get both Portland newspapers every day on her way home from work and devour the news. She would look for news of the USS Alden, but never saw anything. She would occasionally walk to the Crest Theater in the Columbia Park neighborhood, not far from where she lived, to watch a Saturday afternoon matinee. Sometimes she would go with a girlfriend from work, but most of the time she went alone. Helen did not want any complications in her life, and some of her friends from work were high-maintenance ladies, meaning that they demanded a lot of time and attention. Helen did not have the extra energy or the desire to become involved in other people's activities or problems. She was aware of some talk about what would happen to them when the men came home from the war.

Some of the girls were concerned about how they would deal without a job. They were told when they were hired that their jobs were only temporary, but they didn't feel like it was temporary. They had been going to work every day since they were hired, and it was more like a permanent job.

Helen's job at Continental Can Company was what was keeping her on an even keel right now. She was so worried about David, but because of the nature of her job, she had to be 100 percent concentrated on her work at the office. She was able to put her worries about David in the back of her mind while she was at work. Helen worked with figures: numbers of cans ordered, number of cans delivered, amount of metal to purchase to supply the military services with the number of cans they needed. Helen knew the exact number of cans that could be manufactured out of a sheet of tin.

Her supervisors knew that she was doing an excellent job and that she was extremely accurate in her figures and her ordering. They were very rarely over or under their quota with the ordering she did. The only time there seemed to be an error was when the military made a mistake on the numbers they needed. The logistics of the military had to agree with the logistics of the companies they were working with. The whole process was extremely complicated and needed personnel who could do the work and knew what they were doing. Helen was one of those people.

Right now, her job meant everything to her. She was making a good wage and was able to live on that very comfortably and bank all of David's pay that was sent to her. She was sent most of his pay directly and assumed he was able to have some money when he was in port. He had arranged all of that before he left for Hawaii and his first assignment.

David was a Seaman 1st Class. Helen received $50.00 per month from the military, which was his pay when he first went in as a Seaman Apprentice. She assumed that he was making a higher salary now than in early 1942, but that he was drawing some of that pay for his own use. Helen had a little over $600.00 in the bank. When David came home, they would have a nice nest egg to fall back on. Her salary was enough to pay the rent and utilities and to buy what food she needed. She usually had a little left over for a movie with her girlfriends or a soda at the local Woolworth's soda fountain. The only clothes she had bought since David left were what she needed for work. She had to have special shoes, pants, and a jacket. She made do with only one pair of shoes and one jacket along with two pairs of slacks during the entire time she had been working there. She saw no reason to purchase more. Some of the girls that worked in the plant had multiple pairs of pants, several pairs of shoes, and two or three different jackets. As far as Helen was concerned, it was a total waste of money. Her sights were set on what she and David would have when he got home.

Helen often would sit on her sofa at home and wonder what it would be like to have him home again. She knew that the other ladies at work thought about having their men home also. The only difference was that she did not talk about her personal life. The other ladies did.

When the men went off to war, the women had to pick up the slack at home. They had to learn to do the banking and pay bills. They had to learn to navigate the complexities of maintaining a household, most often with small children, and they had to learn how to maintain their vehicles. Even though they couldn't always get gasoline because of rationing, they had to keep their cars in good working order for their husbands.

Willard Martin was very proud of his daughter for the drive that she had to do a good job for the company she worked for, but was worried about her after the war was over and the men came home and wanted their jobs back. He didn't think that she realized that the job she was doing was only temporary.

All of the women who had taken over the jobs that their menfolk had left behind were going to be out of work when their husbands, fathers, sons, or boyfriends returned. They would be delegated to the homemaker status that they were before the war. Both Marian and Gloria, Willard's two other daughters, were looking forward to being home again. They had children in school while they were working or at Grandma's house after school and on holidays and didn't have to worry about childcare, but Helen had nothing but David. And what if David was damaged in some way, either physically or mentally? Would he be able to work in the shipyards the way he did before? Willard didn't know and was concerned about his youngest daughter.

Helen knew in the back of her mind that her job would not be hers once Alex Smith, the man she replaced, returned after the war was over, but she didn't want to think about it. What would she do all day when David came home and went back to work? Without a job to go to, she had nothing to do. She probably would not be hired back at Sears. She didn't want a sales job anyway. She was no good at it. She needed something that would stimulate her mind and keep her busy all of the time. What a dilemma! She imagined that a lot of the women workers were thinking about the same thing.

It seemed that 1943 offered more names of places in the Pacific to remember: Tarawa, Attu, Admiralty Islands, Bismarck Sea were all names that were becoming all too familiar to Helen and almost anyone who had loved ones in the Pacific. 1943 was proving to be a long and frustrating year. There was not a lot of good news coming from either side of the war, Europe or the Pacific.

It was the beginning of 1944, and the United States had been in the war since the end of 1941. That was a long time. Several of the women at the plant had husbands, fathers, or brothers who were already back from Europe. They had been injured and were at home in military hospitals in the United States. They had taken leaves to go visit their loved ones, but all came back to work, needing the money they were making to live on. Their future looked bleak at this point. Helen noticed that there seemed to be an air of uncertainty around the plant, but she didn't want to think about it. She wanted to enjoy her job while she still could and wait for David to come home.

She was receiving more consistent letters from him now. He still couldn't talk about where he was or what he was doing, but she did know that he still loved her and was anxious to get home to her. She knew that time does funny things to the mind, and she was afraid that David would not love her anymore. He assured her in his letters that he did and that he wanted to come home to her.

Marvin Swenson was Helen's immediate boss. He was very pleased with the job she was doing but was not one to give compliments on a job well done. The office had a contest set up where each employee had a specific quota of cans they wanted to make. These quotas had to fit into the parameters of the number of cans that were needed in the inventory. Helen did not participate in the contest because she set up the quotas for the whole company and did not feel it was fair that she should know ahead of time the quotas needed. Both Helen and Marvin were very strict about the total number of cans made. They were more concerned with the bottom line and making sure that the company did not overextend and have a large inventory left unused. When the war was over, they would have to switch back to making cans for private packing plants as well as the military, and they wanted to make sure they did not have an excess inventory of the military-sized cans.

Marvin was aware that Helen's job was just temporary. When the war was over and the men started coming home, they were going to want their jobs back, and the women would have to go. He was going to be sorry to lose some of them. They were good workers, got to work on time, and worked until the job was done. There was very little complaining about the conditions they had to work in, as was not the case with the men. The men complained all of the time about having to work with women and about having to share their break room with the women and about the women talking all of the time. They said there was no peace and quiet, that they got the constant talk at home, and now at work too.

Chapter 7

$\mathcal{H}$elen was concerned about David's parents. They would not talk to her over the phone, and when she did drive by their house, the blinds were shut tight, and it looked like no one was home. A couple of times, she went to the door to try and talk to them, but there was no answer to her knock.

She had gone to one of the neighbors once, but they offered no information about the Cunninghams. She was baffled as to what to do.

One Sunday afternoon, she asked her dad to go with her to their house to see if he could get them to answer the door. She knew that they must be there. Alice's flower garden was well tended, and the lawn was mowed. There were no papers piled up, nor was there mail in the mailbox. During the summer months, she noticed that their upstairs bedroom window was open. She saw the window curtains blowing in the breeze coming in.

They took Willard's car, thinking that maybe they would not recognize it and that they would answer the door.

Roger Cunningham did answer the door when Willard knocked. He just stared at Willard for a moment, then said, "What do you want? Hasn't your daughter done enough?"

"What do you mean? What has Helen done to hurt you?" Willard asked.

"She talked our son into joining the Navy, and now he is probably dead at the bottom of the Pacific Ocean someplace," Roger surmised.

"That is ridiculous. She just got a letter from him yesterday. He can't tell her where he is, but he is fine. Helen did not talk David into joining the Navy. In fact, she begged him not to go. What makes you think she forced him to join the Navy? Did he tell you that?"

"No, he didn't, but we know her type. She just wanted to take advantage of the fact he would be gone and she could do anything she wanted to. That's the way most young women are nowadays," Roger stated firmly.

Willard could hear Alice in the background telling Roger to close the door on him.

All of a sudden, Alice stepped into the doorway. Willard was shocked when he saw her. Her hair was totally grey, and she looked sick. She had lost a great deal of weight.

"I would not look like this if she had not forced him to leave. He would be here to look after me. He always looked after me when he was little," Alice mumbled.

"Come, Alice, go back to your chair," Roger told her.

"I have to go now," he told Willard.

"Is there anything we can do to help?" Willard asked.

Roger shook his head as he closed the door on Willard. "Something is very wrong with your mother-in-law. She acts like she is losing her mind, and she looks awful. She has lost a lot of weight, and her hair is almost all grey now," Willard said to Helen as he returned to the car.

"I haven't wanted to write to David about any of this because I didn't want to worry him or put any pressure on him about his parents, but I think I had better say something," Helen commented.

"You probably should. I think Roger would have said something to me had Alice not come to the door. He obviously did not want me to see her looking the way she did," Willard said.

"I'm not really sure what I will say to David. I guess just tell him what has been going on and explain to him that I did not want to worry him by saying anything sooner," Helen said to her dad.

After dinner at her parents' home, Helen went home and wrote a long letter to David explaining the situation with his parents and why she had not said anything sooner. "Have you heard from them, sweetheart?" Helen wrote. "Does your mother write to you? I love you, David, and miss you so very much. I can't wait for the day you come home."

Helen sealed the letter and went to bed alone for another long night.

Helen woke up the next morning to her phone ringing. It startled her and shocked her even more when it was Roger Cunningham on the other line.

"Alice would have a fit if she knew I was calling you, but I do not believe she is being fair to you. You are David's wife and deserve to know what is happening. Could you meet me for coffee when you get off of work today? You are still working at Continental Can, aren't you?" Roger asked.

"Yes, I am, and yes, I will meet you for coffee. I get off of work at 5:00 PM. I take the bus home. There is a diner about a block away from the bus stop. I could meet you there. It's called the 'Corner Café.' I can meet you there about 5:20," Helen explained.

"Yes, that will be fine. I know where it is," Roger answered. "I will see you there."

Helen was nervous all day waiting for her shift to be over and meeting her father-in-law at the café. She drove the car to work that day because she wanted to be sure to be on time to see Roger.

As she walked into the café, she noticed that Roger was already there. He stood up to greet her, giving her a brief hug as she slid onto the bench opposite him. She was a little surprised at the outward sign of affection coming after so long without any contact at all.

"You are looking good, Helen. You seem to be doing okay with David gone," Roger commented.

"If you mean I am eating, sleeping, and working, I guess I am doing okay. But in any other way, I am not doing okay. My husband is not here with me, and I do not like it, but I can do nothing about it right now. I am functioning to stay alive and be a whole person when he comes home," Helen stated firmly. "I would like to know why neither you nor Alice has wanted to see me since David left. That is almost two years ago. Have you written to him, or is he left out in the cold too?"

"Alice writes long letters to him every day. That is about all she does now. She is losing weight, her hair has turned grey almost overnight, and she has no energy to do anything around the house. I do all of the cooking and housekeeping now. I also tend the garden and flower beds. She wants nothing to do with any of it. She tells me that when David comes home, she will be a whole person again, but until then, she has nothing to do with anyone else. She is totally self-absorbed with her grief," Roger explained.

"I don't understand why she is blaming me, though," Helen said. "I did not want him to leave either and begged him to stay. I was even naïve enough to think he could go back down to that recruiter and tell him that he had made a mistake."

Roger chuckled at that statement. "I am sure Alice wanted to do the same thing, but instead, she just turned cold inside. Now, she has convinced herself that David won't come back."

"I am sorry, Roger. I tell myself a hundred times a day that he will come back to me. I have to believe that or I would go crazy," Helen stated firmly. "Does David write to you? Does he know about his mother and what her condition is?"

"Yes, we do get letters from him. I'm sure not as many as you do, but he writes. He doesn't say much. I'm sure he can't. I have some friends who have gotten letters that are blacked out in places, so we know that the mail is censored. Alice does not write to him. She says the letters will just go into a dead letter box and he won't get them. I write about once a week, and yes, I have told him about Alice and about her attitude towards you and how she blames you for him being gone," Roger explained.

"I haven't said anything for fear he would be worried about that and not concentrate on his job," Helen explained. "Now that I know he is aware of the situation, I can say something to him. Thank you, Roger, for saying something to me. I appreciate your confidence."

"Let's meet on a regular basis, Helen. I do not want there to be a rift between us. I have to believe Alice will eventually come around. I am sorry I waited this long to talk to you. I was trying to do what Alice wanted me to do," Roger stated.

"Thank you, Roger, for explaining all of this to me. I want to make sure that David doesn't think that I have just abandoned the two of you because he is gone. I really have tried to keep in touch. Apparently, I have tried at a time when you were not home. My dad figured that you would not recognize his car if he drove to your home. And yes, let's meet again soon. You two are my family also, and I do not want to lose touch," Helen said as she got up to leave the café.

Roger gave her another brief hug as they stepped outside. Helen watched him walk to his car with a sadness in her heart.

David was his only child, and all of his hopes and dreams for the future were tied up in him. Helen had to be realistic and know that there was a chance that he would not come home from this damn war. What would Roger and Alice's life be like then? She and David had not even given them a grandchild before he left. She shook herself to come back to reality and walked to her car. She decided to drive to her parents' home instead of going to her place first. She wanted to talk to her dad and mom. And she wanted to get rid of the idea that David would not come home.

Some of the ladies at work gathered after work once a week to talk about their situations and what would happen to them when their men came home. Once in a while, Helen would attend these get-togethers and listen to what the girls had to say. A lot of their talk was about what their sex life would be like when the men came home. Helen was surprised at how easy it was for some of the women to talk about their personal lives. Helen was a very private person and did not talk about her life with David, even to her mother or sisters. But the girls brought up some valid issues about how they would adjust to giving up the responsibilities of paying bills, taking care of the house and yard, and raising the children. They had a lot of questions and did not know where to go to get the answers.

At one of the meetings during the lunch hour that Helen did attend, the women were complaining about not having any place to go to get the answers they needed when Helen spoke up and said, "Have you ever thought of contacting the Red Cross? They might have someone who can help to answer some of your questions."

One of the girls from the production line spoke up and asked, "Is there a branch of the Red Cross in Portland?"

Some of the other ladies laughed at the comment. "Honey, there is a branch of the Red Cross in every city in America, I think. Why don't you look it up in the phone book and give them a call? They just might have someone who can give us some information about how we are to react and what we should do when our men come home. Personally, I do not want to give up this job. I like working and having my own money. I don't have any kids to take care of, so I am free and easy. When my man comes home, I hope to keep on working. Maybe not here, but someplace," she explained.

Another young girl said, "Okay, I will call the Red Cross and see if we can meet with someone from there who can answer our questions."

There was a branch of the Red Cross that provided counseling to both returning military personnel and to their families. Mae, the young girl charged with getting the information needed, made arrangements for a representative to come speak to them after work the next week.

Chapter 8

$\mathcal{E}$xcept for the fact that David was not home, the year passed very quickly. Helen was working extra hours at the plant trying to keep up with the orders for cans to be packed. The packing plant was in Northwest Portland, and the finished cans were sent over to them via truckloads several times a day.

The Allies were making a little headway in Italy, but for every advance forward, there seemed to be a push backward by the Axis troops. Reading the newspapers and listening to the news on the radio was at times discouraging, but everyone listened and read anyway. The war news was addictive.

The war news in the Pacific wasn't much better. The fighting on Guadalcanal was still going on, but the reports were that it was just a "clean-up" operation. Unfortunately, there were still a lot of casualties being reported from there. The scary thing for Helen was that they reported losing ships. The battle of the Philippine Sea was finally reported as a great victory for the Americans in June of 1944. The Island of Guam was taken back by the Americans in July of 1944.

Despite some discouraging news about ships going down and high casualties, Helen continued to have hope that the war would be over soon and David would come home. She had started going to church on Sundays. One of the women she worked with had invited her to go to the Methodist Church not far from where she lived. At first, she was self-conscious about being there. She did not go to church when she was growing up, and she and David had not established themselves with a church yet. They were married in her parents' backyard with a judge performing the ceremony.

But once she got used to the routine of the service and what to expect, she became comforted by the message and the caring of the people there. The message given was always uplifting, and prayers for the servicemen and women were always lifted up. She felt a peace when she walked into the church now.

Her parents were a little shocked at her church attendance. It was something they never did, and they had not raised their children in a church environment. Helen had invited them to attend with her, but they declined every time she asked.

On June 6, 1944, news came over the radio that the Allies had just invaded France on the beaches of Normandy. June 6th was a Tuesday, and the news came over the loudspeaker at work. All work stopped so that the employees could listen to the reports on the radio. It was reported that the Allies had amassed the largest water invasion in military history. At each new announcement over the radio, cheers went up over the whole plant. There was absolute silence when General Eisenhower came on the radio and announced the invasion.

Whether the employees of Continental Can believed or not, the management asked for a moment of silence in commemoration of the invasion. Helen believed that this was the beginning of the end for the Nazis.

Even though the war was not over in the Pacific, it seemed that some of the sailors and marines were coming home. Unfortunately, they were the injured ones. They were coming into the San Francisco Port of Embarkation and being sent to hospitals from there. Most of them went to the Letterman Military Hospital at the Presidio in San Francisco. They were equipped to take the most severe injuries.

Most bodies of the dead servicemen were sent to the National Cemetery in Honolulu, Hawaii. The families had a choice to have them sent to the states to any cemetery they wished. Helen knew that David had updated all of his paperwork to make sure that she was the person notified if he should be killed in battle. She had decided that if David was killed, she would have him buried at Willamette View Cemetery in Southeast Portland. It had a fairly large area for military burials, and she wanted him close.

Most of the time, Helen tried to shake off feelings of David being killed in battle. She tried to assure herself that he would come home safe and sound.

She knew that there was a possibility that he could have some mental issues when he was released. She didn't know, but she knew that there was the possibility that he had seen people die and it might affect him mentally.

At the request of the employees, the company had someone come from the Red Cross to talk to the ladies about what would happen when the men came home from the war. They sent two volunteers out who talked about the men coming home and what they would need from their wives, mothers, sisters, and girlfriends. They did mention that it might be hard for them losing their jobs, but it would be best if they returned to their pre-war routine as soon as possible. Being a housewife and mother would be the best thing for the returning men so that they could assimilate into their environment in an easy and familiar manner.

Helen thought that was kind of the opposite of the type of advice they needed. They needed to know what would make the transition easier for them. They had been pretty much independent women for four years now, doing things and making decisions for and by themselves. What would be the emotional toll on them when the men came home?

Helen spoke up and asked that question of the volunteers, but they seemed to turn it around to make it the wife's job to make things easier for the men. Helen asked if the returning men were given a talk on how they could make it easier for the women. The Red Cross volunteers did not answer the question but went on to talk about fixing the men their favorite meals and giving them the attention that they needed. As far as Helen was concerned, the meetings were a waste of her time.

The newspapers were reporting a new weapon that the Japanese were using on the American fleet. They were called kamikazes. The Japanese men would deliberately fly an airplane into a ship, usually causing an explosion and fire and hampering the ship's ability to fight back.

Helen and her friends could not understand the mentality of someone who would deliberately commit suicide like that. The ladies talked a lot about how the Japanese would adjust after the war. They knew it was a given that the Americans and the Allies would win the war. The only question was when it would happen.

In December of 1944, news was broadcast of a battle in Belgium between the Germans and Americans. The weather was terrible, and planes could not fly, so the ground troops had no air cover. The Germans completely took advantage of the weather and started a ground offensive to push the Americans back.

When the weather cleared enough for the planes to fly, the Allies pushed the Germans back, and thanks to some reinforcements and clearer weather, were able to push them towards Germany and advance towards Berlin.

In the Pacific, 1945 started out with the Americans landing on an island called Iwo Jima. The news on the radio and in the newspapers was pretty discouraging at first. The Japanese were pretty well dug into the island, hiding in caves and raining fire down upon the Americans with abandon.

Helen was afraid most of the time now for David's safety. With the kamikazes raining havoc on the ships in the area, the possibility of a ship being hit and the crew being hurt was greater than usual.

The girls that Helen worked with were tired of the war too. They wanted to go out and buy new clothes, get a new pair of shoes, have enough sugar, meat, and eggs without having to figure out how many rations stamps they had and whether they could buy something in the store. They were tired of the stores being out of everything all of the time. And they were tired of not being able to drive their cars without worrying about whether they would run out of gas and not having enough ration stamps to get some more.

On April 30, 1945, news came over the radio that Adolf Hitler was dead. He and his wife, Eva Braun, had committed suicide. Then on May 8, 1945, it was announced that Germany had unconditionally surrendered and the war in Europe was over. There was great rejoicing all over the United States at the news. That meant that the troops would be coming home.

Unfortunately, the war was still raging in the Pacific. But it was felt that with the war over in Europe, more of the resources could go to end the Pacific War.

Helen had to readjust some of her inventory figures to reduce the number of cans going to the European Theater of War. There would still be troops there for a while that would need to have rations, but certainly not as many. She would have to contact the logistics department at Fort Lewis, Washington, to readjust some of her figures.

In June of 1945, when school was out, Helen and her sisters decided to pool their gas ration stamps and take the kids to the beach for a weekend. They hadn't been away from Portland for almost four years and needed the break. They decided to take Helen's car because it was the largest and would be more comfortable for the four ladies and three kids to ride in. The trunk was full of sleeping bags and food, and Willard Martin had tied a couple of suitcases to the back of the car.

Helen did the driving. David was pretty fussy about his car, and she wasn't sure he would approve of someone else driving it. They headed for Seaside, Oregon. Willard knew of a small set of cabins there that the girls could stay in. They would all cram into one room, but they didn't mind. All they wanted was to get away and see the ocean.

The weekend was relaxing for all of them. No one slept very well, but that didn't matter. The kids dug in the sand, and the girls lay there and soaked up the sun.

Helen explained to her nieces and nephew why there were so many ships on the horizon. They were there to protect them. The Navy and the Coast Guard were patrolling the coastline to make sure no enemy ships came too close.

The kids all thought that because Hitler was dead and Germany had surrendered, the war was over and their daddies would be coming home. Helen tried to explain to them that only half of the war was over. The other half, where their daddies were, was still going on.

There was a lot of talk among the women at work about what would happen to their jobs when the men came home. It was the consensus of all that they would probably be out of work. Some of them were not at all happy about it. They loved working and wanted to continue to do so. Hopefully, the plant would have other jobs that they could do.

Helen was sure David would not be happy having her work around a bunch of men. When she was at Sears, she was working with other women, and the only time she came in contact with the men at the store was in the general store meetings, and then she always sat with the girls. The men worked in the hardware, plumbing, large furniture, men's suit department, and large appliance departments. They were not involved with the ladies or children's clothing department where Helen worked.

She didn't want to go back to Sears to work, but if that was the only place she could get a job, she would. She did not want to commute to downtown Portland to some of the bigger department stores. She would have to transfer buses to get to work on time. Sears was a straight shot down Grand Avenue from her house. All of this would depend on what David was going to do. If he was going back to the shipyards, he would want the car, and she would have to take the bus.

Helen was really getting ahead of herself, though. David was not home, and she did not know what his plans were. He hadn't expressed them in any of his letters.

Chapter 9

About the end of June 1945, some of the men started coming back to Portland from the European campaign and came into the office to inquire about their jobs. They were assured that their jobs were there waiting for them when they were ready to return to work.

The women who had done those jobs for the past four years were summarily laid off. They worked on a Friday and were told that their job was over, given their final paycheck, and told not to return on Monday. It was a harsh way to be told, and the ladies were not happy about it at all. They had been faithful employees of the company for four years, and now to be told on Friday not to return on Monday—now what would they do? Their husbands were still on some godforsaken island in the Pacific Ocean.

When the men came back, there were still some women on the assembly lines, and the men resented them being there.

One of the men shoved a woman out of the way, saying that she wasn't doing the job correctly. He bruised her arm badly when he shoved her, and she went to management to complain. They didn't know what to do except move the lady to another area on the line. She was told that her job would end when the man that she replaced came back, so it didn't make sense to make a big fuss about it.

Several of the women were incensed at the attitude of management, so they decided to speak up during the lunch hour. The woman who was shoved got up on a chair and asked for the attention of the people in the lunchroom.

"I want you all to know that we are very glad that you men are coming home alive and that you will be able to have your jobs and your lives back, but we also want you to know that we did your work while you were gone to keep you from starving. Where in the hell do you think all of the K-Rations came from? You certainly were not here to make the cans. We did it. We kept track of how many were needed and when they had to be shipped out. We cut the metal to the right size and put those cans together. Maybe we weren't as strong as you, and maybe it took two of us to move a pile of tin, but we got the job done. So, don't just shove us out of the way. Unfortunately, we know that we must leave our jobs when the soldiers return, but we did get the job done."

The women in the lunchroom stood up and clapped, and the men just sat there. About two minutes later, one of the men got up and clapped and was followed by all of the rest of the men.

One of the men got up to speak: "It is hard for us to comprehend what you ladies went through while we were gone. Working outside of your homes was not something that we were used to having our wives and mothers doing. But we do want to thank you for keeping our jobs going for us and providing us with the products that we needed. We know that all over the country, women went to work in the plants and factories and shipyards. We do appreciate it and don't mean to put you down for the job that you did."

Everyone continued to clap and cheer, and finally, people went back to their jobs.

Helen was curious as to how long her job would last but was afraid to ask. She guessed it would depend on when David came home. The last she had heard; his ship was somewhere near the island of Okinawa. According to the map, that was very close to the main islands of Japan.

Helen continued to do her job, but her heart was not really in it now. She wanted David home, and she wanted to get back to a normal life, whatever that was.

She occasionally heard from her father-in-law Roger. Alice was not getting any better. David had sent her several letters telling her that he was okay and would be home soon, but she did not respond to them. She was convinced that Helen had killed him by sending him off to war. Nothing that Roger or David would say could change her mind.

On Monday, August 6th, the loudspeakers came to life in the office. Helen was trying to concentrate on some figures and was annoyed by the interruption. An announcement came over the loudspeaker that the U.S. had just dropped an atomic bomb on the city of Hiroshima on the southern island of Japan.

"What in the world is an atomic bomb?" Helen said to no one in particular.

"I don't know," someone else said.

Another man spoke up and said, "It is the bomb that could end this damn war."

The loudspeakers were left on with the news reports continuing. Helen tried to get back to her column of figures she was processing, but it was difficult. Her fear for David was great. Was he nearing this terrible bomb? Was he still alive?

Finally, she couldn't take the noise anymore and told her supervisor that she was not feeling well and went home early. She had never done that before, but she was too nervous to keep working.

Helen drove to her parents' home. She knew her dad would not be home from work yet, but her mother would be there, and she wanted the comfort of her family right now.

Jane Martin had the news on the radio when Helen walked in. "What are you doing here at this time of day?" she asked her daughter.

"I left work early. I couldn't stand the constant noise and chatter, and I am frantic about David right now. You don't suppose he has anything to do with the dropping of that bomb, do you?" she asked her mother.

"From the sound of it, sweetheart, no Allied ships were in the area at the time. It would have been too dangerous for them. The bomb was dropped from high up in the air, and the plane that dropped it got away very quickly. From what I have heard on the radio, the devastation was immense. Many civilians were killed. I guess it was dropped to make the Japanese realize that we mean business when we say the war is over. Apparently, the powers that be feel that too many of our men will be killed if we try to invade Japan proper," Jane explained to Helen.

"Mama, I just want David home," Helen cried in her mother's arms.

"I know, honey. Hopefully, he will be home soon," Jane answered.

Helen had dinner with her parents that evening and then went home to her apartment. There was a letter from David waiting for her in her mailbox. She grabbed it and had it opened up before she got into the house. She sat down on her sofa to read it. "Sweetheart, I want to let you know that the Alden was hit by a torpedo yesterday. I am okay, but have a pretty bad gash on my leg. I am on a hospital ship headed back to Pearl now. They stitched my leg up but said I would need some additional surgery and therapy when I got home. It looks like it won't be long now. They say that I will be transferred to Barnes Medical there in Vancouver after they do the processing in Pearl. I don't know exactly when that will be, but I will let you know. They will fly me from Pearl to Portland Airport, then transfer me by ambulance to Barnes," David wrote.

Helen sat there and cried, then called her parents to let them know what David's letter said. She also called David's parents' home, hoping that Roger would answer and not Alice. Roger did answer the phone, and Helen read him the highlights of David's letter. Roger was grateful for the information but couldn't say very much because Alice was sitting right there.

He said to Helen as she was hanging up, "Thank you for that information. I will take all of that into consideration."

"Who was that on the phone, Roger?" Alice asked.

"Just a salesman wanting to sell me siding for the house. He says now that the war is almost over, we will have the supplies to fix up our homes again," Roger answered. He hated to lie to his wife, but it was best in this case.

"But the house doesn't need new siding," exclaimed Alice.

"I know that, dear, but I was just trying to be polite to the man. He is trying to rebuild his business, and it is not an easy task," answered Roger.

"When David comes home, he will reside it for you if it needs it," Alice stated firmly. "He will be living here and will be available to help us all of the time."

"Alice, I have told you before, David will not be living with us. He is married, and he will live with his wife, Helen."

"No!" Alice yelled. "He will not live with that woman. She made him leave us, and I will not allow my son to go back to her. She is evil."

"Alice, don't say that to David. You will never see him again if you do. He loves her and will return to her."

"I will not allow it! I will not allow it!" Alice mumbled as she walked into their bedroom to lie down.

Roger just shook his head, not knowing what he was going to do about her. She was getting worse all of the time. Now she was refusing to bathe or get dressed. She kept saying when

David got home, she would take a bath and put on some nice clothes. She didn't think it was necessary until then.

Roger wasn't able to open the doors or draw back the curtains while Alice was in the room. She wanted it dark and stuffy, she said, until David came home. Then we could open the curtains and door again.

He was going to have to get tough with her pretty soon. She was acting more bizarre all of the time, and he didn't know what to do about it. Maybe he would call the doctor and ask him to make a house call. He knew that it would be almost impossible to get her to go to his office.

Roger made sure that Alice was asleep, closed the bedroom door, and went to the kitchen to call her doctor. Doctor Tim Jacobs had been Alice's doctor for over 20 years and had become a good family friend during that time. He had lost his wife several years ago, and Alice and Roger had invited him to dinner several times to give him a good home-cooked meal.

Roger explained the whole situation to Tim and asked if he could make a house call to assess her situation. He arranged for him to come over the next evening, the 9th of August. Tim said he would bring dinner for the three of them.

The day that Doc Jacobs was to visit the Cunninghams, the news broadcasts were full of reports that the United States had dropped another atomic bomb. This time the bomb was dropped on the city of Nagasaki, again killing and maiming thousands of civilians. Doc called to see if Roger still wanted him to come. Roger said that Alice was getting worse daily and he needed some professional help. He couldn't cope with her any longer.

He had said nothing to Alice about David being hurt and on a hospital ship sailing back to Pearl Harbor. He was afraid that would put her over the edge completely.

The doorbell rang about 5:30 in the afternoon on Thursday, the 9th of August. As usual, Alice was in her dressing gown and had not washed or combed her hair. She was waiting for Roger to fix her some dinner and was getting frustrated because he wasn't getting up to do it. Roger went to the door and greeted the doctor with a very grateful handshake and ushered him into the living room.

"Good evening, Alice," Doctor Jacobs greeted Alice fondly. "I haven't seen you for a while or been over for one of your delicious meals, so I thought I would bring supper with me this time and treat the two of you. How are you?"

"I am not sick, if that is what Roger told you," Alice said to him curtly.

"No, he didn't say you were sick, just that you were down in the dumps a little and might need a pick-me-up," Doc answered.

"I will be just fine when David gets home. He has been gone a long time and needs to be home. He will help Roger put new siding on the house when he gets here," Alice announced.

"I kind of figured that David would go back to his home with Helen when he comes home," Doc said.

"Absolutely not!" Alice screamed. "Why does everyone say he will go back to that woman? She is the one who forced him to go away in the first place. Why would he want to go back to her?"

"Well, Alice, they are married and probably want to resume their married life together," Doc said very frankly.

"I will not allow it. Do you hear? I will not allow him to go back to her. He is my son and belongs with me now and forever. He doesn't need anyone else," Alice announced.

"Let me put this food into the kitchen, and we can set the table and eat," Doc said as he motioned for Roger to follow him into the kitchen.

"How long has it been since she bathed? She smells terrible," Doc asked Roger.

"I can't remember the last time, to tell you the truth. I have started sleeping in the other bedroom. I can't stand the smell, and she won't let me open the doors during the day to get some fresh air. If I do open them, she comes along behind me and slams them shut," Roger explained. "I tell you, Doc, I am at my wit's end."

"Does she really think that David will move back in here? Does she know that he is injured?" Doc asked.

"Yes, to the first question, and no to the second," Roger answered. "I haven't told her about David being injured. I was afraid it would put her over the edge completely."

"It might," Doc said. "Let's eat this while it is still relatively warm. I stopped at the deli and picked up chicken dinners for the three of us."

Roger went into the living room to get Alice to come to the table, but she was not there. He checked her bedroom and found her curled up in bed.

"Please come and eat with us, Alice. Doc was kind enough to bring a nice chicken dinner over for us. It would be nice to enjoy it together and to thank him for it," Roger pleaded with her.

"No! I am not going to eat anything more until David comes home," Alice stated firmly.

Roger gently closed the door of the bedroom and went back into the kitchen to tell Doc what she had said.

"If she refuses to eat, I will have to hospitalize her and put a feeding tube down her throat. She won't like that at all. Do you want me to tell her that?" Doc asked.

"Yes, by all means do. She needs a swift kick in the butt as far as I'm concerned," Roger answered.

Doctor Jacobs went into the darkened bedroom where Alice was lying curled up on the bed. As he came into the room, he turned the light on so he could see her.

"Turn the damn light off, Roger. You know I don't want the light on," she yelled.

"It isn't Roger. It is Tim Jacobs, and I want the light on so I can see you. Why are you acting like this, Alice? This is not you. You have always been a bright, vibrant lady with energy to spare. Why now?

"I will be fine as soon as David gets home. I will do nothing until he does. He will come back to me when he comes home. She can't have him anymore. Enough is enough!" Alice stated very firmly.

With that statement, Doc Jacobs explained to her exactly what he would do if she stopped eating. He would send her down to Salem to the Oregon State Hospital for evaluation and request that they put a feeding tube down her throat so that she would get some nourishment.

"Doc, that will never happen. David will not allow his mother to be put away in an insane asylum. It just won't happen," Alice said.

"David won't have anything to say about it. It will be court ordered," Doc countered.

"Well, I just won't go. No one can make me do anything I do not want to. Ever!" Alice answered back.

Chapter 10

Apparently, the bombing of Nagasaki finally caused the Japanese to realize that they could not win the war, and they surrendered on August 15, 1945. They signed the surrender papers on board the USS Missouri in Tokyo harbor on the 9th of September 1945. The war was finally over. All over the world, there were celebrations. Stores were closed, and there was dancing in the streets of even the small cities. Now people waited for their loved ones to come home.

Helen knew that David was at the hospital in Pearl Harbor, but there was no word as to when he would be sent home. Roger had called her to let her know what was happening with Alice.

"The doctor is getting papers signed now to place her in Oregon State Hospital in Salem. Helen, she has truly gone off the deep end. She is convinced that everything will be okay when David comes home and moves back into his old bedroom. She is thinking of him as a little boy again. She hasn't eaten any solid food for over a week, and I can't get her to bathe or clean herself up. She just says that when David gets home, she will take care of it," Roger explained to her.

"Roger, I am so sorry. I wish there was something that I could do to help, but I am apparently the problem as far as she is concerned. I have talked to David a couple of times on the phone, but have not said anything about how severe her condition is. I just told him that she is not feeling well," Helen explained. "I don't want him to worry about anything right now but getting his leg healed and being able to come home to me."

"That is as it should be, my dear. You concentrate on your husband and yourself. How much longer are you going to be able to work?" asked Roger.

"Alex Smith, the man I replaced, will be back next week, so Friday the 24th will be my last day. I will miss working. I have loved that job and learned so much. I wish there would be places that the women could work, but most of the returning soldiers don't want us there. They want it to be the way it was before they left for the war. There were quite a few of the workers who were killed, and their jobs could be open, but management says that they will fill them with returning soldiers who do not have jobs waiting for them," Helen explained.

"Well, I'm sure David will enjoy having you around for a while."

"To tell you the truth, I am a little scared about seeing him again. It has been four long years. A lot of the fellows were able to come home on leave or their wives were able to meet them in Hawaii, but we were not able to do that," Helen admitted.

"You will do fine. Just enjoy being together again," Roger said softly.

Helen's last day of work at Continental Can Co. was the 24th of August. She didn't really want to leave. She liked her job, and according to everyone there, did a very good job of it. She wasn't sure what she would do with her days now. She didn't want to look for other employment not knowing when David would be home or what he would want her to do. This was all totally new territory to her. She had worked since she and David were married and had rarely taken a vacation. The trip she took to the beach with her sisters and nieces and nephew was the closest thing to a vacation she had had for years. What would she do with her days?

Both of Helen's sisters were waiting for their husbands to come home too. They had both been in Europe and were still on duty in Germany. Her sisters had no idea when they would be home. Her brother had been in the Pacific and was due home sometime in the latter part of September. It would be good to have the whole family together again.

Helen's dad, Willard, was very proud of his grandchildren now. They were polite, well-mannered young people after a couple of camping trips with their grandfather. Their fathers would be very proud of them when they saw them. And their mothers had changed their thinking on how to raise their children. They saw what a disruption their behavior was before their grandpa got ahold of them.

Helen left work on that Friday with a heavy heart. She had taken very little personal stuff to the office with her, so didn't have a whole lot to carry home on the bus with her. She said goodbye to all of her co-workers and Marvin Swenson, her immediate boss, and left the building to walk to the bus stop. Marvin was sorry to see her go. He knew he could depend on Helen's work to be accurate and concise. He wasn't sure about Alex Smith anymore. A lot had changed in four years. But there wasn't much he could do about it. Alex was entitled to his job back.

Helen had tears in her eyes as she boarded the bus for the last time. She put her token into the box when the driver noticed that she was crying.

"Are you okay, Helen?" he asked. The regular driver knew Helen pretty well. She rode almost every day for the last four years.

"My last day of work today," Helen mumbled to him. "I will miss coming to work every day."

"We will miss seeing your smiling face every morning and evening," he declared.

Helen walked the short distance from the bus stop to her front door with a heavy heart. She was hoping that a letter would be waiting for her from David. As she looked in her mailbox, she was disappointed that there was no letter from him, but as she put her key in the lock and opened the door, the phone started to ring. She raced to the kitchen to answer it. It was David calling from Pearl Harbor.

"Hi sweetheart. I don't have a lot of time to talk, but wanted to let you know that I board a plane at 5 o'clock tomorrow morning for San Francisco and will be home on Monday, the 27th. They will transport me directly to Barnes, so don't bother going to the airport. Just go to Barnes, and I will see you there. I am so excited to hold you in my arms again. Wear something pretty. I love you," David told her.

"Oh David, that is so great. I will be at Barnes bright and early in the morning on Monday, waiting for you. I love you too and will see you soon," Helen said to David as she heard someone in the background yell, "Hey, Cunningham, get off the phone."

As she hung up the phone, she started to cry again. She not only cried for her lost job but for the joy of her husband coming home.

Helen put her things away and decided to use some of the sugar she had to make David some of his favorite chocolate chip cookies. Most rationing of food and gasoline were stopping with the ending of the war, but sugar was still being rationed, so Helen wasn't sure when she would get some more, but David was worth it.

After making her cookies, she decided to do a thorough cleaning of her house. It had been a while since she had done a deep cleaning, and she wanted everything to look perfect for David. She knew he would have to be in the hospital for a while, but this was a good time for her to clean. She would put some music on and get down to the real cleaning.

Helen liked the 1940s big band music for easy listening, but she also liked classical music. She put on a record of the 1812 Overture, turned it up loud, and got to work. She started on the kitchen first. It took her two hours to clean the refrigerator, all of the cupboards, counters, stove, and oven, and mop the floors. Then she proceeded to the bathroom and gave it a good cleaning and disinfection. It smelled so much better after she was done. It was 9:30 PM by the time she finished the bathroom, and she was exhausted. The bedroom, hallway, and living room would wait until tomorrow.

Helen spent the entire weekend cleaning her house. She was not sure when David would be able to come home, but she wanted it clean for him when he did walk in the door again.

She took all of his civilian clothes over to her parents' house on Sunday and put them into the washing machine there. She did not want to spend the money to do them in the laundry room at her apartment building. She was able to wash and iron all of his things, and after supper, took them back to her apartment and put them neatly back into his drawers. She also moved some of her clothes back to her side of the closet so that he would have more room.

Finally, on Sunday evening, she felt she was ready. Her house was spotless, his clothes were clean, and in the morning, she would take a long bath, wash her hair, put some makeup on, and get herself ready to see her husband for the first time in four years. And she was scared to death. What if his tastes had changed? What if he decided he didn't love her anymore? What if he had met someone on leave that he wanted more than he did her? All of these thoughts were going through her head as she was driving to Barnes Military Hospital in Vancouver, WA. For Helen, it was closer to drive across the bridge to Vancouver than to go to the VA Hospital in Southwest Portland. All she had to do was get on Highway 99 and cross the interstate bridge, and she would be in Vancouver.

Helen parked her car in the visitor parking lot at the hospital. She slowly walked into the building and up to the information desk. After explaining why, she was there, the lady at the desk excused herself and went into an office behind the desk. In a few minutes, an Army doctor came out carrying a folder full of papers.

"Mrs. Cunningham, would you please follow me into my office? I am Captain Ronald Walker, a doctor on staff here at Barnes. Please sit down," he said as he pulled out a chair for Helen.

"What's wrong, Doctor? Did something happen to David?" Helen asked in a panicked voice.

"Mrs. Cunningham, your husband fell in his hospital room in San Francisco and reinjured his leg. He broke it in two places and has undergone surgery to try and repair the breaks. On top of the other injuries to his leg, it does not look good," the doctor said.

Helen started to have a hard time breathing and was having a panic attack. She was afraid she would faint.

The doctor came around the desk and pushed her head down. "Breathe deeply, Mrs. Cunningham. You will be fine," Captain Walker said. He buzzed his receptionist and asked her to bring a glass of water in to Helen.

After taking a drink of the water and composing herself a little, she asked, "What happened? How did he fall?"

"Apparently, your husband was trying to get out of bed by himself. Somehow, he slipped on the floor and went down onto his bad leg. The staff heard him scream and ran into his room to find him on the floor in extreme pain," the doctor explained. "What do I do now? How long is he going to be there?" Helen asked.

"We are not sure. He will be undergoing therapy in San Francisco for a while before he can be sent up here. The leg will have to be stabilized before they will put him on a train home," the doctor further explained.

"I thought he would be flown home," Helen said.

"Unfortunately, no. The train is the preferred method of transporting non-life-threatening injuries. Mrs. Cunningham, would you like to go to San Francisco to see your husband?" the captain asked.

"Sure, I would, but I cannot afford a trip to San Francisco," Helen stated firmly.

"I think I can arrange for you to have a train ticket down there and put you up in the visitor's quarters on base. Do you have someone, a relative maybe, who could go with you?" the captain asked.

"I could ask my mother, I suppose. My two brothers-in-law just got home last week, so I am sure my sisters would not want to leave right now," Helen answered.

"Your mother would be included in the trip as a companion to you. The military is not keen on women traveling alone right now. There are too many men home now and at loose ends. Could you call your mother and ask her? I could make the arrangements right away if that would be okay. You can come into the conference room to make the call in private if you would like?"

"Thank you very much," Helen said very quietly.

After speaking to her mother and explaining the whole situation, her mother was excited about a trip to San Francisco with her daughter, even if it was under stressful circumstances.

As Helen walked back into the captain's office, she had a smile on her face. Dr. Walker was pleased with the way she looked. "Mrs. Cunningham, I will make the arrangements for you and your mother to leave on Wednesday, August 29th. You will take the train to San Francisco Station and will be met by a car from the Presidio Medical Center. They will take you to the visitor's quarters, check you in, and then direct you to the hospital where your husband will be waiting for you. I will need your mother's name and address for the train tickets. You will be able to spend 10 days in San Francisco. Hopefully, by that time, your husband will be ready to come home. He will not be able to come on the same train as you, but hopefully, he will follow very soon."

After giving the captain the information he needed about her mother, she left the hospital and drove back across the bridge and straight to her parents' home.

Chapter 11

W illard Martin drove his wife and daughter to the Portland Train Depot on Wednesday morning and saw them board the train for San Francisco. He was excited for them to have this trip together and for Helen to get to see David. It would take about 19 hours to get to San Francisco. Willard made sure that both of them had plenty of money to be able to eat in the dining car without having to watch their pennies. He had heard that the service on the Seattle to Los Angeles run was excellent, so the ladies should have a great time.

Both Helen and Jane were nervous as they boarded the train. They found their seats and were pleased to note that they were only two cars away from the dining car, so the walk would not be a long one. They were able to put their overnight bags at their feet, and their larger luggage was stored in a special bin close to the door. They would carry it off themselves as they got off at San Francisco.

The countryside was beautiful in Oregon and Northern California, and the ladies thoroughly enjoyed the trip. The food was very good, and the service excellent. They made stops in several cities along the way to pick up and drop off passengers and pulled into San Francisco early on Thursday morning. Helen and Jane were both able to freshen up before they had to leave the train. A driver was waiting on the platform with a sign that said "Mrs. Cunningham" and took them to the visitor's quarters at the Presidio Medical facility. It was an exciting drive through the heart of San Francisco, and by the time they reached their destination, they were exhausted from looking at all of the sights.

After checking in and getting into their room, Helen inquired about visiting David at the hospital. It was a short two-block walk to the area where David was.

Jane was going to stay in the room while Helen saw David for the first time, but Helen wanted her mother with her. She could wait outside David's room if she wanted to, but Helen wanted her close. She was scared. She had been anticipating this meeting for so long.

As she went to the nurse's station, she was directed to David's room. The nurse said that he was asleep but should wake soon. Helen was allowed to go into the room at any time she was there. She did not have to observe visitor hours. As she walked into the room, she noticed that there were five other patients in the room with him. His bed was curtained off and was the only patient that was sleeping. The other soldiers made comments as she passed by. "You're as pretty as he said!" came from one bed. "Are you the private's woman?" and a simple "WOW!" from the third bed. The fourth and fifth beds were quiet except for a whistle that came from one of them; Helen wasn't sure which one.

As she went behind the curtain, she saw David lying there with a tube in his arm and his left leg propped up in a sling of some kind. He had a bag hanging under the end of the bed that his urine ran into, and he looked so very uncomfortable that Helen broke into tears. She sat down in the empty chair, took his free hand in hers, and whispered, "I'm here now, sweetheart."

David slowly opened his eyes and looked at Helen like she was a stranger. "Why are you here? You are supposed to be at home waiting for me. I don't understand why you are here."

"Mother and I are both here. They sent me down to spend some time with you, and my mother is here as my companion because they did not want me to travel alone. I am here for ten days, David," Helen explained.

"You should not have come. I didn't want you to see me like this," David said as he turned his head away.

Helen was crushed at David's words. "But David, I am your wife and I have wanted to be with you so badly. I love you."

"Just go, Helen. I don't want you to see me like this. I can hardly move, let alone put my arms around you and hold you. Just go back to Portland. I will see you when they send me home," David ordered in a louder-than-usual voice. "Just get out of here, please."

Helen stood up with tears streaming down her face and left the room. The other men were very quiet as she left. She heard one of the men say as she left, "Cunningham, you are one stupid jerk."

Jane was surprised to see Helen come into the waiting room crying. "What is the matter, sweetheart?" Jane asked as she stood to put her arms around her daughter.

"Mama, he doesn't want me here. He told me to go home and he would see me when they let him come home. He doesn't even want me in the room," Helen sobbed on her mother's shoulder.

"You sit down here, and I will get you a glass of water," Jane told her. She came back into the room with a glass of water and told Helen that she was going to speak to David, that she would be right back.

"No, Mama! He will only be mean to you too," Helen begged.

"I can take it. Sit, and I will be back," Jane said.

She walked into David's room and up to his bed. She pulled back the curtain and said to her son-in-law, "How dare you talk to your wife that way! Do you have any idea what she has been through in the last four years and what she has sacrificed for you? She has gone without personal comforts, without the companionship of her husband or his family. Your mother has treated her like shit for four years. She kept that from you because she didn't want you to worry. You have no right to talk to her like that. When you married her, you said, 'for better or worse, in sickness and in health, 'til death do us part.' Now is the time to take those words seriously. I am going to send her back in here, and you WILL apologize to her. Willard and I love you too, David, and we are very sorry you are hurt, but we also love our daughter and will not see her hurt by you or your mother."

Jane turned around and left the room to the claps of the other patients.

David hadn't said a word. He just lay there and stared at his mother-in-law, stunned at what she was saying. What right did she have to talk to him like that? He was a veteran of the war. He deserved better than that. But thinking about it, he realized that he didn't deserve better than that. He got the talking-to that he deserved for the way he talked to Helen. His Helen, she was so beautiful. How could he have forgotten what she meant to him? He loved her so much and wanted to be tall and strong for her and to be able to hold her in his arms and make love to her the way they used to. He couldn't do that now with his leg strung up like it was and all of these tubes in his arm.

A nurse came in to check on the IVs in his arm and to make sure his leg was properly positioned in the sling. Helen slowly walked back into the room and saw the nurse there checking on David's leg and rushed to his bedside to make sure all was well. The nurse assured her that his leg was fine and that the doctor would be in momentarily to check on him.

"Thank you very much," Helen said very quietly, all the time looking at David, who was avoiding looking at her. After Jane's tirade at him, he was very embarrassed at his actions and attitude.

When the nurse left the area, David looked at his wife and said, "Can we start this greeting over again?"

"I would love to," Helen answered as she leaned down and gave David a very tender kiss on the lips.

David deepened the kiss, then buried his face in her neck and started to cry. "Oh God, how I have missed that and missed you. Maybe I will come alive again with you here. I feel like I have been dead for four years, just acting like a robot or something. I have missed you so much. I'm sure the memory of your sweet kisses has kept me alive these past years. I am so sorry for my actions earlier. I had dreamed of standing on the dock after leaving the ship and having you run up to me and throw your arms around me, and we would run off to a motel and make love for hours. When that didn't happen, and with me confined to this bed and not able to move, I was crushed and didn't want you to see me looking like this. Your mother's little speech drove some sense into me," David explained. "Is she still outside? Would you ask her to come back in?"

Helen nodded and went out to get her mother. Jane followed her daughter back into the room, where she saw David with a smile on his face.

"I am so sorry, Jane, for my actions earlier. It was unforgivable of me. I was so distraught at the fact that I couldn't hold her and give her the greeting that I had dreamed of, that I tried to turn her away. I am profoundly sorry that I treated her that way and that I treated you as badly. You are the best mother-in-law a guy could have," David stated.

"Thank you, honey. I appreciate your apology. Now, I am going to walk back to the room and take a nap. I am tired, and when I wake up, Helen, we maybe can go out and get something to eat," Jane stated.

"Okay, Mama. You rest, and I will see you later," Helen said.

The hospital staff arranged for Helen and Jane to have a car available along with a guide/driver to show them around. They were very keen on taking care of the dependents of their wounded servicemen. In the ten days that Helen and Jane were in San Francisco, they were able to see Fisherman's Wharf, Nob Hill, and Chinatown. They were given a tour of the Presidio, along with being driven across the Golden Gate Bridge. They saw the infamous prison, Alcatraz, from a distance and saw some of the large troop transports coming under the bridge, bringing the men home from war.

Helen was able to spend about four hours a day with David. Between therapy appointments and his rest time, that was all the time she had with him, but she savored each moment.

One afternoon towards the end of her stay, David asked Helen to tell him about his mother. She explained what had happened and the fact that she did not tell him sooner because she did not want to worry.

"I was sure she would come around, but she never did. Your dad and I had coffee one day and he explained her situation to me, but she has only gotten worse. She finally gave up taking care of herself. She would not bathe, eat, or do anything around the house. The doctor came to visit and told her that if she didn't start eating, he would have to put a feeding tube down her throat, but that didn't seem to faze her. Your dad finally had her sent to the hospital in Salem. I talked to him just before Mother and I left, but she has not improved. She says she will eat again when you come home to live," Helen explained.

As the ten days were drawing to a close, Helen was becoming more and more depressed at the idea of leaving David, but he assured her that he was doing well and would be home soon.

As she was leaving his room on the next-to-last day she was there, David's doctor stopped her and told her that it should be about two weeks and he would be ready to come home. Since she assured the doctor that there were no steps that David had to climb to get into their apartment, he said that David would probably be able to come directly home. A few adaptations would have to be made in the house, but she could have those done in a very short time. Her heart started racing when she realized that he would come straight home and not go to Barnes Hospital in Vancouver.

Helen and Jane both went for a last visit on the evening before they left. Helen had tears in her eyes, but David assured her that it would not be long and reminded her that he would be coming directly to their home from the train station.

The nineteen-hour train ride back north to Portland was long and tiring for both women. Jane was anxious to get home to Willard, and Helen was anxious to get started on the modifications needed to their apartment so that David would be comfortable.

Chapter 12

Helen contacted her landlord regarding the changes that needed to be made. She needed a ramp on the front of the house so David's wheelchair could get to the front door, and she needed a lift on the toilet so that David could use it comfortably and not risk the danger of falling.

To Helen's dismay, the landlord refused to give her permission to make the changes. He said that he did not want the eyesore of a ramp in the front of his house. She offered to pay for the changes herself, but he still refused.

"But without those changes, my husband will not be able to come home," Helen cried.

"Sorry, but I just can't have you making those changes. I understand that his parents have a ramp at their house. Let him go home to them!" the landlord said.

Helen looked at him with fire in her eyes, whirled around, and drove to her in-laws' home. She saw the brand-new ramp up to the front porch of their house and noticed that the entry door had been widened to accommodate a wheelchair. As she stared at the house, Roger Cunningham walked out onto the front porch and looked at her.

"Alice arranged for this work to be done. She is home from the hospital now and seems to be doing much better knowing that David will be coming home soon. Unfortunately, Helen,

Alice says that you will not be welcome in our home. She says that she has talked to David and he will be filing for a divorce as soon as he gets home."

Helen was in a state of shock but aware enough to drive to her parents' home. She sat in the car until Willard finally came out to see what was wrong.

"Daddy, they won!" she said.

"What do you mean, they won? Who are you talking about?" he asked his daughter.

"David's parents won," she said as she sobbed into her father's shirt.

When she was able to talk clearly, Helen explained what had happened with her landlord and the changes made to the Cunningham house.

Willard immediately got on the phone and made a long-distance call to David in San Francisco. "I can't believe that she did that," David stated. "I have not talked to her at all. Please let me talk to Helen, Mr. Martin," David asked.

Willard passed the phone to Helen, saying, "He wants to talk to you!"

"David, she's won. She won't let you come home to me. She has fixed their house so that you have easy access to everything and talked our landlord into refusing to let us modify our place. And she won't let me see you while you are there. I don't know what to do," Helen sobbed.

"Calm down, sweetheart. I am not going to their house. You and your parents look around for another place. Talk to a realtor if you have to. There should be houses to rent that can be modified on a temporary basis. I love you, honey. We will be together soon, I promise. Just know that I will not be moving into my parents' home at all," David reassured her.

"Thank you, honey. I will talk to you as soon as Dad and I find something. We will start looking today. I love you," Helen said as she hung up the phone.

"Dad, will you and Mom go with me to find another house to live in that we can modify for David?" Helen asked.

"Sure, honey! We can go right away," Willard said as he looked at Jane for confirmation. Jane was already at the closet getting her jacket on.

The first thing Willard did was drive to a realtor's office in the St. John's area of North Portland. Mr. Richard Barber was a prominent realtor in the North Portland area and was a casual acquaintance of Willard's.

Willard explained the whole situation to Richard and asked for his help in finding Helen and David a place to live. He went through his card file and found three places that would be ideal for David and Helen to live in. They were all fairly close to bus lines and the local shopping area. And it was an easy commute to the shipyards when David was able to go back to work.

He took Willard, Jane, and Helen out to look at the houses. The second house that they looked at was vacant, and they were able to go into it right away. It already had a ramp up to the front door. Richard explained that this place was a "rent-to-own" house, meaning that the rent paid would go towards a down payment on the house, and eventually, David and Helen could own the house. The only difference would be that none of the utilities—electricity, water, sewer, etc.—would be included in the rent. They would have to be responsible for it all.

Helen was sold on the property. The house was a small one-story bungalow with two bedrooms, but it did have a basement for storage and room for a washer in the basement. The interior of the house needed some work, cleaning, and painting, and a couple of the windows needed to be replaced, but all in all, it was in good condition. Willard checked out the oil furnace and the roof to make sure they were in good condition. They would need to have a refrigerator and stove, but they could be purchased in good condition at a second-hand store.

Helen had not told David, but she had been very frugal in the four years that he was gone and had almost $4,000 saved in an account at the bank. She had saved all of his military pay that she received, living only on what she made at Continental Can.

Richard explained to Helen that this house would not be available for very long. There were a lot of people looking for housing right now, and it would be snatched up very quickly. Helen made a snap decision and told Richard Barber that they would take the place. She paid a small deposit to hold it until she could call David and let him know. She did not want to lose the house.

David agreed with the rental of the property, and Helen went back the next day and paid the full first month's rent. She was handed the keys right away and drove over to the house to walk through it on her own.

She explained to David that she would paint the interior of the house right away and arrange to have all of their belongings moved in within a week.

"It might be kind of jumbled right away, but I will get everything straightened out in time for you to come home. I can't wait for you to see our new home. We even have a yard, and I can plant a flower bed and garden. Oh David, I am so excited about this place!" Helen exclaimed.

Helen worked all day, every day on painting the interior of the house. Her dad helped her in the evening when he was home from work, and her mom came over when she could during the day. Helen chose bright, airy colors for the kitchen and living room and a soft green for the bedroom. Willard had to do some plumbing work in the bathroom but was able to fix everything himself without having to call a plumber. Willard did find out that they would have to replace the water heater eventually, but Helen was not worried about that now. She just wanted to have everything ready for David. He was due to come in on the train next week, and according to his doctors in San Francisco, would be able to come directly home if the house was wheelchair ready.

Willard managed to commandeer the sons of a couple of his friends to help move Helen and David's belongings into the new house. Jane had a couple of spare rugs stored in her basement and gave them to Helen to use in the living room and bedroom. The carpets in her rental belonged to the landlord.

Helen and Jane made sure that the rental that Helen was moving out of was in pristine condition. She wanted her $25 damage deposit returned. The landlord was not happy about returning it but could find nothing wrong with the place that warranted keeping the $25. Helen was very happy to be out of there, considering the attitude of the landlord.

Helen had all of the utilities and the phone hooked up at the new house and canceled at the old one by the time her furniture was moved in. She walked into the house with a load of clothes when she heard the phone ringing. She dropped the clothes on the sofa and ran to the kitchen to answer the phone, thinking maybe it was David. Instead, it was Alice Cunningham on the line.

"You will not get away with this," Alice exclaimed.

"Away with what, Alice?" questioned Helen.

"You know. Moving so that David will move into your place. It will not work. He will be coming home, and that will be the end of it," Alice stated firmly.

"No, Alice. That is not the end of it. David and I are married, and we will not be getting a divorce. He will be moving into our new home when he returns to Portland and will not be coming to your home. Your home is not his home any longer," Helen said.

"If I have to, I will get the authorities involved. We will see what happens to you then," Alice said to Helen.

"Alice, the authorities will do nothing. David and I are legally married and have been for six years now. You do not have a leg to stand on," Helen answered.

Alice slammed the receiver down on the phone, and Helen just laughed. Alice had really gone off the deep end now, thinking the police could do anything about keeping her and David from living in the same house.

When David called that evening, Helen explained to him what his mother said.

"She has really gone berserk, hasn't she?" David commented. "I will talk to her when I get home. She has to understand that I will not live with them again. Have you talked to Dad?"

"Briefly, but there seems to be nothing he can do. She appears to be okay health-wise, and the doctor will not put her in the state hospital unless she does something to harm herself. And she won't do that as long as she thinks you will be coming home to her house. Your dad is at a loss as to what to do," Helen explained.

"Don't worry, sweetheart. I will take care of it when I get home. I can't wait to see our new home. It will be so nice to have a yard and flowers and a vegetable garden in the spring and summer. Maybe we could get a couple of chickens and have fresh eggs. Oh, and maybe, if we can fence the yard, we could get a dog. I have always wanted a dog, but Mom never let me have one. She said they were too dirty," David rambled on. "Yes, as soon as you get home, let's get a dog. I will ask Dad about possibly fencing the backyard. It shouldn't cost too much, and I have saved a lot of money over the past four years," Helen said.

"Is there a garage?" David asked.

"No, but there is a covered area to park the car right next to the house. It has a concrete floor, and there is a small storage shed right at the back of the concrete area. We could keep garden tools in there," Helen explained.

"I can't wait to see it!" David exclaimed. "Only one week left here, then they will send me home."

"I'll be ready, sweetheart. You have a good night's sleep, and I will talk to you soon," Helen said as she hung up the phone.

Helen finished unpacking her car and made the bed so that she could spend her first night in her new home. Willard had changed all of the locks for her and installed security bolts on the three exterior doors, so she felt very safe spending the night there.

At 2 AM on Tuesday, the 25th of September, Helen's first night staying in her new home, she was awakened by glass shattering in the living room. She was scared but went into the kitchen and called the police to report someone was breaking into her home. They advised her not to go to the front of the house and to wait, that they would be right there.

When the police car drove up to Helen's house, they found Alice Cunningham, in her nightgown, throwing rocks at the front window of Helen's house. She had shattered the large window and put a crack in a smaller one beside it.

There was a knock on the door, and a voice informed Helen that it was a police officer. Helen opened the door to find Alice Cunningham standing there with a policeman holding onto her arm. "Mrs. Cunningham, do you know this lady?" the policeman inquired.

"Yes, I do. That is my mother-in-law, Alice Cunningham," Helen said in a flat voice. "She said she would get the authorities involved in our dispute. I guess she has now."

Another policeman took Alice to the police car and placed her in the back seat. Helen invited the other policeman in and explained the whole story to him.

"Should I call my father-in-law?" Helen asked.

"No. We will do it from the station. You might want to have that window boarded up first thing in the morning, ma'am," the policeman suggested.

"I will, and thank you for being so prompt," Helen answered.

When she closed the door and locked it, she went to the kitchen and called her father. It was 5:30 AM by that time, and she knew he would be up.

Willard went right over to Helen's, looked at the damaged window, took some measurements, and said that he would take care of fixing the window that day. He knew how to replace windows and would get one of his friends to help him.

Chapter 13

With the windows replaced and the glass cleaned up, Helen decided she had better call David and let him know what had happened. After explaining to him what had happened the night before with his mother, Helen said, "You probably should call your father, David, and find out what has happened to your mother. Of course, I will not press any charges. I just want her to get some help and face reality. She doesn't seem to want to face the fact that you and I are married and have been for six years."

"I am so sorry you have to go through that alone, honey. I will call Dad and see what's up. She will probably be put back in the hospital in Salem. Mom has always been somewhat possessive of me, but never to this extent," David commented.

"It started when you left to join the Navy. She blamed that on me. It was when you left that she would have nothing more to do with me," Helen explained. "I feel sorry for your Dad, having to deal with all of this by himself."

Helen hung up from talking to David. She had to rehang the living room curtains and drapes. They had been taken down to replace the windows.

After she had finished with the curtains and drapes, she looked around and found everything was in order. She had a few things to pick up at the grocery store, but other than that, she had nothing more to do. What would she do for the rest of the day? She had no job to occupy her daytime hours. What did women do during the day when their husbands were at work to keep themselves busy? She didn't have children, so she couldn't use that as an excuse. She supposed she could look for a job, but what's the use? David would be home in another week and she would be busy taking care of him. She would probably have to drive him back and forth to therapy and to doctor's appointments when need be.

Maybe she could learn to sew, but she didn't have a sewing machine, and who would teach her? Her mother didn't sew. Her mother wasn't clever at doing any type of needlework. She could barely sew a button on. Helen always did that for her.

While David was gone, she had started going to the Methodist Church in St. Johns. Maybe she should join the women's group there. Someone there might be able to teach her to sew, or knit, or crochet, or something to keep her busy. She decided to go to church on Sunday and see when the women's group met.

On Sunday morning, Helen dressed in her good suit, put on a hat and gloves, and went to church. She was a little shy but was greeted warmly by the usher and led to a seat about halfway down the aisle. She sat next to an older couple who quietly greeted her with smiles and handshakes.

The service was lovely, and she truly enjoyed the music. Maybe she could join the choir. She had sung alto in her high school choir and still had a pretty good voice. It would be fun to sing again. There was a coffee hour in the social hall after the service, and as Helen walked in, she was greeted by several women. They made her feel so welcome, she almost wanted to cry.

"Hello. My name is Helen Cunningham. Thank you so much for the lovely welcome. I do so appreciate it. My husband is in the hospital in San Francisco but is due home next week. I worked all of the time he was overseas but find myself at loose ends now and am looking for something to occupy my time. I thought maybe there was something here at the church that would give me an opportunity to do some good in the community instead of just sitting around," Helen explained.

"Oh, I know there is something we can find for you," one of the ladies said. "Do you knit or crochet?"

"No, neither one. I would like to learn, though. I will be taking my husband back and forth to physical therapy and doctor's appointments and would like to have something to do to occupy myself as I wait for him," Helen answered.

"You have come to the right place, my dear. We have a class on Wednesday evening at 6:00 PM for beginning knitters, crocheters, and embroiderers. You would fit in perfectly. We usually start you out making dishcloths. They are easy and very useful. All you would need is a couple of crochet hooks or knitting needles, whichever you want to learn to do, and a skein of yarn. We can teach you from there. We have printed instructions to help beginners get started. Can you be here at the church at 6:00 on Wednesday?"

"Yes, I will be here, and thank you so much. This will solve a big problem for me. I am not used to being idle. My house is as clean as it is ever going to be. The floor will start wearing away if I scrub it anymore," Helen said, laughing.

One of the other ladies looked at Helen oddly and said, "Cunningham! Are you related to Roger and Alice Cunningham?"

Helen sobered quickly. "Yes, they are my in-laws. Why, do you know them?"

"Yes, they used to go to church here before the war started. Then they quit coming. We tried to contact them several times to make sure all was well, but we never had any response from them. We kind of figured they had left the area," the woman explained.

"No, they are still here," Helen stated. "Alice has not been well since David left to join the Navy in 1942."

"Oh, I am so sorry to hear that. I will send her a get-well card right away," the lady commented.

"It would probably be best if you didn't mention that you met me. She and I do not have the best of relationships right now. It would only agitate her more if she knew," Helen told them.

"Ladies, thank you so much for the kind welcome and the invitation to join you on Wednesday evening. I will be here with the necessary supplies in hand. I am expected at my parents' home for dinner soon, so I must be on my way," Helen said as she turned around to leave.

Helen had a pleasant dinner with her family. She told them that she went to church that morning and about the invitation to the Wednesday evening classes.

"I am excited about learning to crochet. I think I will do that instead of knit. Knitting takes two needles, and to crochet, you only need one hook. It might be easier. If I can learn to do this, it will give me something to do while I wait for David at his therapy appointments. As I understand it, he will have three appointments per week to start with, then they will take them down to two, then to one as he progresses. They will be working him hard, but that is good," Helen told her family.

Helen's sister's husbands had been home for a couple of months now and were back to their pre-war jobs. The girls were getting used to having them back but sometimes complained about the fact that they seemed to be taking over everything. The girls had been doing for themselves for four years and were having a hard time letting go of some of the chores and allowing their husbands to take over. They were used to disciplining their children, and now their husbands were doing it, and it was hard to let go. The children were also having a hard time.

When Helen's brother-in-law, Josh Timms, told his daughter Laura to do something, she refused, and he slapped her across the face for talking back to him. Gloria, Helen's sister, had to talk to her daughter and explain to her that her daddy was back from the war now and he had a say in what happened in the family. Apparently, according to Helen's mother, Josh went off to the bar to have some drinks with his buddies from work.

Gloria was confused about how to handle the turmoil that Josh's return was causing. She was concerned about the children and how they were dealing with the changes. Both of them were acting up and having problems in school. They were glad their Daddy was home, but didn't know how to deal with the changes.

Things were not much better with her other sister, Marian. She was having some difficulty adjusting to her husband being home and taking over also. Both girls were undecided as to how to proceed and what to do, except let their husbands have the final say. They certainly were not used to it, and the men were not that way before they went off to war. The twins were also having trouble. They had grown up a lot in the four years their Daddy had been gone. They were identical twins, and Michael could no longer tell them apart. It frustrated him, and the girls were taking advantage of it. They would do something out of line, and their father would correct them, not knowing which daughter they were correcting. Their mother finally caught on to what they were doing and sat them down for a long talk about respecting their father and helping him get used to being at home again and getting used to them.

Marian and Gloria were able to talk to their children and explain how hard it was for their Daddy to come back from the war, but who could they talk to about their frustrations?

"I hate to see this happening to them, Mama," said Helen one afternoon when her mother was at her house visiting. "It makes me happy that David and I don't have any children yet. When we do, we will be able to raise them together."

"That is the best way for sure," Jane said. "What do you hear from David?"

"He is delayed another week. The doctor wanted to make sure that he was able to move from the bed to his wheelchair without falling. I am so disappointed. I want him home right now!" Helen asserted.

"How is your crocheting class going?" Jane asked her daughter.

"I have only been there once, but Mrs. Bremer was very kind in showing me how to crochet a chain. And I was able to read the directions and make a row of single crochet on top of the chain. Let me show you what I have done so far," Helen said as she pulled out her crocheting from a bag by the sofa.

She had five rows done and was very proud of her work.

"It's a little crooked, isn't it?" her mother asked.

"Yes, and I'm not sure what I did wrong. I will go back next Wednesday evening, and Mrs. Bremer will tell me, I'm sure," Helen laughed.

Jane got up and went into the kitchen to pour them another cup of tea while Helen worked a little bit on her crocheted washcloth. "What do you hear from Roger?" she asked Helen.

"Not a thing. I am afraid he is too embarrassed to speak to me. David said to just wait. He has talked to his Dad and will settle everything when he gets home. I know he is going to want me to drive him down to Salem so he can see his mother and talk to her personally," she explained.

"Both of them need to see each other. Hopefully, she will calm down when she sees him," Helen said.

When Jane left that afternoon, Helen fixed herself a sandwich for supper and went into the living room to listen to the radio and do some more crocheting. She really enjoyed seeing the progress of her work, but it really was crooked.

As she was working on her piece, the phone rang. She got up and went to the kitchen to answer it. The call was from her father-in-law, Roger. "Do you know yet when David will be coming home?" he asked.

"Not exactly. He was supposed to come home this week, but the doctors want to make sure he can transfer from his bed to his wheelchair without any problems before discharging him. David was adamant about coming directly home and not going to Barnes in Vancouver," Helen explained.

"Okay. I will let Alice know. She was concerned about him and wanted to know why he isn't home yet," Roger commented.

"Roger, where is Alice? Is she at home with you, or is she in Salem in the hospital?" Helen asked.

"Well, she is at home right now," Roger said nervously. "She convinced them at the hospital that she was fine and that she had to be here when David came home."

"Roger, David is not coming to your house. He is coming to our new house, and that is final. I am really getting mad, Roger. You tell your wife to butt out of David's and my life. He is my husband and will be coming home to me, not your addle-brained wife."

Helen slammed down the receiver of the phone and sat at the kitchen table crying. Boy, the war had screwed up everyone's life.

Chapter 14

Helen was afraid that Alice would try to do something to her house again. She called David to let him know what his dad had said. David was getting more and more concerned about his mother and what harm she would be capable of doing. He wanted to get home to Helen. It was his job to protect her, even if it was from his mother.

Helen felt better after talking to David, but was still worried about the house. She called her mom and dad and they immediately came over. They brought some extra clothes in case they had to stay overnight.

Helen didn't sleep very well that night. She gave up her bed to her parents and slept on the sofa in the living room. She had a small cot in the spare bedroom, but it was piled high with stuff she had to put away. There were some noises outside during the night, but every time Helen looked, she could see nothing.

Willard was the first one up in the morning and he went to the kitchen to make coffee. He looked out the window in the dining area of the kitchen and saw that someone had dug a very large hole in the side yard. The dirt and sod were scattered all over the lawn and it looked terrible.

"Helen, wake up, dear," Willard said as he touched Helen's shoulder. "Wake up. There is something you have to see outside."

"Do I have to get up, Daddy? I didn't sleep very much last night. There were noises, but every time I looked, I couldn't see anything," Helen yawned as she talked to her father.

Jane walked out of the bedroom wearing one of Helen's dressing gowns. "Sorry!" Jane said. "I forgot to bring one."

"That's okay, Mama. Daddy was just about to show me something outside. Like I told him, I heard funny noises all night, but every time I looked out the window, I couldn't see anything amiss," Helen explained to her parents.

As they walked out the side door of the house, Helen saw the large hole in the side of the yard and the mess strewn around the hole. It looked like someone had thrown garbage into the hole and around the yard. It was a mess and there was a large hole in her beautiful lawn. Willard had just mowed it for her and she had worked one afternoon to get the flower beds all weeded and pretty looking for David's homecoming, and now this.

Helen assumed that it was Alice who had done this or hired someone to do it for her. Roger had said that she was at home, but Helen doubted that she would do something like this herself. She wouldn't have wanted to take the chance of getting caught again and going back to jail.

If it was Alice who did this, she was going to press charges, mother-in-law or not. This was vandalism and it would take time and money to clean it up, fill the hole in, and reseed it. It would be summer before it looked decent again.

"Oh my," Jane said. "What a mess!"

"I am calling the police," Willard said. "This is vandalism and the police need to know about this."

Helen was standing there with tears rolling down her face. "I don't understand it. I have done nothing to her, or anyone else as far as I know. All I have done is marry her son and love him. She never indicated before he went into the Navy that she didn't like me. I know she didn't want him to go into the service, but good God, I didn't either. He went because he had to. I didn't understand it then, but I do now."

Both Willard and Alice put their arms around her and led her back into the house and closed the door on the mess. Willard went to the phone and called the police. They were at the house within a half hour.

After taking the report, asking a lot of questions, and referencing the previous vandalism report, the police gave Helen some names of companies that would help with the cleanup and restoration of the lawn.

It would cost her some money to get the lawn repaired, but she would call her insurance company and place a claim for the damage. She knew that she had a deductible, but that was okay. She thought it was about $50.00.

Within two days, the garbage was gone and the hole in the lawn was patched. The lawn maintenance company that the police had recommended did a great job of putting the pieces of sod back and reseeding around that sod. They put a wire fence around the area and said they would be back to check on the progress within a week.

Helen was very pleased with the work that they did mainly because she heard from David and he was to board a train the next day and be home on Thursday, October 4th.

"Are you sure there will be no more delays this time?" Helen asked.

"I am sure, sweetheart!" David answered. "I told them I would come back and haunt them forever if there I wasn't on that train."

Helen laughed and gave a huge sigh of relief. She hung up the phone after a few more minutes of talking to David. She decided not to let David's parents know when he was coming in on the train. She did not want them there to greet him.

But the next morning, she received a call from David saying that they had to wait another week because of a train crash along the line in Southern Oregon and it would take that long to clear the tracks.

"Now the date is October 12th. This better be the last delay," David said angrily.

Helen got to the Portland Railroad Depot about a half hour before the train was due in on the 12th. The place was busy, but she walked out to the platform to wait.

There on the platform, she saw Willard and Alice Cunningham along with a medical attendant with a wheelchair beside him. She walked up to Alice and asked what she was doing there.

"I am here to take my son home and there is nothing you can do about it. I have a court order that says that because you are incompetent and not able to take care of him properly, he is to come with me," Alice announced to Helen. Willard just shrugged his shoulders in the background.

"Who in the hell gave you a court order saying that I was incompetent? No one ever talked to me," Helen yelled. "Let me see the order," she demanded.

"I do not have to show you anything. Now leave. You are not wanted here. I will be convincing David that he must get a divorce from you. You are crazy, breaking your window and digging holes in your yard and blaming me. That is ludicrous!" Alice said to her with her head raised slightly and her nose up in the air.

Helen went back inside the terminal and called the police along with calling her father. There were already policemen in the terminal and one of them followed Helen to the platform. The policeman approached Alice and asked to see the court order.

"Why? Why do you need to see it? It is legal," Alice stated.

"If it is legal, Mrs. Cunningham, there should be no reason for you not to show it to me," the policeman said.

"Well, it is in the car. My son will be here very shortly and I don't have time to go get it now," Alice said pleadingly.

"We will make time, Mrs. Cunningham. I will go with you," the policeman said.

"But she will take him away from me," cried Alice. "She can't have him."

"We will deal with that when we get back with the court order. Now, let's go get it so we can get back. Mr. Cunningham, will you please accompany us?" the policeman asked Roger.

Helen couldn't believe that this was all happening, but just at that time, she heard the train coming into the station. She stepped back as the train stopped and she walked to the door that the gate attendant indicated that the wheelchair would come out of. As the door opened, she saw David sitting there dressed in his uniform and with a big smile on his face.

As the attendants set the chair on the ground, Helen ran up to him and gave him a big hug and a kiss and whispered in his ear that his parents were here and that they were going to take him home with them.

"No, they are not. I will not go with them," David said loudly. "Your mom says that she has a court order saying that you have to go with them, that I am incompetent to take care of you," Helen said with tears in her eyes. Helen explained about the policeman and his mother leaving the order in the car and having to go get it.

Just as she said that, Alice came running up to David, threw her arms around him, and tried to sit down on his lap, hurting his bad leg. David pushed her away, trying to protect his leg. His father pulled her away from David while the policeman was explaining to Helen that the court order was a fake and was not signed by any judge that he knew in the city or county.

Just about that time, Alice started screaming that David was her son and that Helen was trying to kidnap him and the policeman wouldn't do anything about it.

"Honey," David looked up at his wife pleadingly, "Please get me out of here. She is really flipping out."

Helen had borrowed her dad's station wagon to get David. She knew that between the wheelchair and his duffel bag he would have, it would not all fit into their smaller car.

As they were driving home, David marveled at the changes in the city in the four and a half years since he had been home. From the railroad station, Helen drove down Front Street and went across the St. John's Bridge and headed east a little way to their new home. She couldn't wait for David to see it.

David was quiet on the way to the house. He knew where the area was from his old paper route when he was a kid, but didn't know the specific house. He was nervous about seeing the home he would live in. Helen had picked it out all by herself. He just hoped that he liked it.

When Helen drove the car into the driveway, David couldn't believe that this was their house. He had delivered papers to this house years before. At that time, it was a rundown house with heavy bushes all around it. You couldn't even see the porch or front windows for all of the shrubbery. It was a beautiful house now. It was white with pretty dark blue trim with the ramp up to the front porch painted a dark blue also.

"I used to deliver papers here," David said in amazement. "It was a real dump then."

"The previous owners had totally redone the whole house. The wiring has been updated and all of the plumbing has been redone. The bathroom fixtures and the kitchen sink are all fairly new, within 10 years I think, the roof is only five years old. The basement has a concrete floor and there is space for a washing machine. I thought maybe we could look around for a good used washer. My dad has strung clothes lines down there for me and there is an area outside for the clothes lines to be put. It only needs the lines put up," Helen explained.

"If you will get my chair up to the door here, I will get into it and push myself up the ramp. It is not a steep ramp and I am strong enough to do it myself," David said.

Helen marveled at the strength in David's arms when she watched him push himself up the ramp to the front porch. She handed him his key to the house and asked him to unlock the door. David looked at her with adoring eyes.

Just then, a rock was thrown onto the front porch, just barely missing David in the head. Helen turned around to look, but the car sped by and she could not even see the color of the car.

"What the hell is going on around here?" David yelled. "Why would someone throw a rock at us? What in the hell did we do to piss someone off so badly?"

"David, I think your mother has hired someone to harass us and to cause us problems. She couldn't have done that herself. She is not strong enough to throw a rock from a moving car. She could not have dug a hole in the side yard either. It was done in the middle of the night. Again, she is not strong enough to do the digging herself. I think she has hired some thug to do it for her," Helen stated. "She wants you with her. She doesn't want you to have anything to do with me. She thinks she can force you to divorce me."

"Do we have an attorney?" David asked.

"Yes, I hired a lawyer to look over the rent-to-own papers on this house before I signed anything," Helen explained.

"Good. I want to talk to him and get a restraining order on my mother and father. He is obviously enabling her to do these things to you and I will not have it. I also want to set up an appointment in the attorney's office with my parents and the both of us. I want witnesses to everything that is said at that meeting," David announced.

"Now, let's get inside this beautiful house and let me see what you have done. By the way, Mrs. Cunningham, I love you very much!" David added.

Helen smiled as she opened the door and let David wheel himself into the living room.

"It is beautiful. You recovered the furniture. It looks great. I love the colors you picked," David commented.

"Those are just inexpensive slipcovers I found for the furniture. It is costly to reupholster furniture and ours probably isn't worth the cost. If we are careful, the slipcovers will last a couple of years and maybe by that time, we will be able to afford some new furniture. I really didn't want to spend the money on things we don't really need right now. I thought maybe a washing machine was more important than new furniture now," Helen said hesitantly.

David wasn't used to being frugal with his purchases. If he wanted something, he usually went out and bought it. He remembered Helen being the same way, but she had changed. She was being careful with their money now. He guessed that was good, but once he went back to work, he would have control of the finances and he would be able to buy what he wanted.

Helen took David's duffel bag into the bedroom while he wheeled himself around the rest of the house. He was really impressed with the way she had decorated the kitchen. There was a fairly good-sized eating area in the kitchen where they could probably get about six people comfortably around their table. It would be fun to entertain their friends again.

Helen had planned one of David's favorite meals for that evening. Spaghetti and meatballs were on the menu. David loved her spaghetti sauce and devoured a huge plate of it. When supper was over and Helen had cleaned the kitchen, she joined David in the living room to listen to the news on the radio.

Chapter 15

------- ◆ -------

There were terrible stories coming over the news about what had happened to the Jews in Europe. A military tribunal was being formed, and trials would start in November. Some of the top-ranking Nazis had been arrested and sent to prison. They would be put on trial in Nuremberg, Germany. Helen almost got sick thinking about what the Nazis did to those people. The people who liberated Poland and Germany had found huge furnaces where they had burned the bodies of the Jews. It was said that they were gassed beforehand and then burned so they would not have the chore of burying all of those bodies. Apparently, there were millions of people killed that way.

Helen got up and turned the radio station to some music. There was a station in Portland that played some of the popular band music, and she really liked it.

"Hey, I was listening to that," David said. "Please turn it back on."

"I just thought that since this is your first night back, we could listen to something a little less depressing," she commented. "Well, I want to stay current on what is going on in the world and want to listen to the news. Turn it back on," David told her.

Helen looked shocked at the way David was speaking to her, but she got up and changed the station back to the news.

"While you are up, you could fix me a cup of coffee. I like to have one before I go to bed at night," David informed her.

"Okay," Helen said tentatively. "Why are you talking to me this way?"

"What way? What's wrong with the way I am talking to you?" David asked.

"You are ordering me around like I was one of your lowly privates in the Navy," Helen explained.

"So, what? It's the way I want to talk to you. Don't fret it. Get used to it," David answered his wife.

Helen fixed David his cup of coffee and put it down beside him, then went into the bedroom to get ready for bed. As she was turning down the bed, David wheeled himself into the room. "You don't need to turn my bed down for me. I can do it myself."

"What do you mean, your bed? This is our bed," Helen said, looking at David with an odd expression.

"I just assumed that you would want to sleep in the other room until my leg heals. I would not want you to kick it or hit it in any way in the middle of the night. That would hurt too much and could cause added damage," David explained.

Helen hesitated for a few minutes and then whispered, "You do not want to sleep with me?"

"Not now. I can't take any chances with my leg right now. It would be best if you moved some of your stuff into the other room. There seems to be plenty of room for you in there. I need the extra room to maneuver the chair around. And, by the way, please don't come into the bathroom when I am in there," David demanded.

Helen went to her dresser, pulled a bunch of her clothes out, and took them into the other bedroom. She made several trips between the rooms, carrying her personal belongings into the other bedroom. She emptied her side of the closet and the nightstand on her side of the bed. She even took the clock and the lamp, as there was none in the other room. She was absolutely livid. She couldn't believe that on their first night together after over four years of being apart, he would treat her this way.

As she was leaving with the last of her things, David said, "I would appreciate it if you would leave me the checkbook. I will be taking over the finances now that I am back."

"I will get it for you tomorrow. I am tired, and it is in among all of the mess in the other room," Helen told him.

"Just don't forget," David added as she left the room and slammed the door behind her.

Helen was so upset she couldn't even cry. She would get up early in the morning and drive to her parents' home. She didn't want to call them now.

Helen retrieved her handbag out of the front coat closet and took it to the spare bedroom. She would have to put all of her things away somewhere. There was no room in the dresser in that room. She had extra linens and mementos stored in it. She would get some boxes and pack some of it up to store in the basement. In the meantime, she hung up in the closet what she could and folded and set her lingerie on a towel on the floor.

Helen didn't have a set of sheets that fit the cot-sized bed in that room, so she folded a double bed sheet in half and put it on there with the only spare blanket she had. She would have to borrow another one from her mother. The nights were getting cold, and she would be cold at night with just a thin blanket over her.

In the middle of the night, Helen heard rustling in the hallway, got up, and opened the door to see if David needed help. He was wheeling himself into the bathroom, and when he said a curt 'no' to her offer of help, she closed the door and sat down on the bed again.

She pulled the checkbook out of her purse to look at the amount of the balance. When she looked at the checks, she realized that David was not a signer on the account. She had changed banks while he was gone. Their previous bank wanted to lower the amount of interest they paid on the balance, and she found another bank that paid more, so she changed. She had forgotten to tell David about it. He would be mad that he couldn't have easy access to their money. She had spent some of the amount that she saved while he was gone, but still had about $2,500.00 left. She was going to take $1,000.00 of that out and leave it with her parents in case she needed any ready funds. She had heard some of the girls talking at church about the returning husbands spending all of the money their wives had saved and the ladies having nothing to buy groceries with and no way to feed their children. Many of the men refused to let their wives go out and get jobs to add to the family income.

It would not be possible for Helen to work for a while. She was needed to drive David back and forth to his therapy appointments.

At 6:30 in the morning, Helen left the house without saying anything to David and drove to her parents' home. They were up having their morning coffee in the kitchen when she walked in the door. They were both shocked to see her there.

"What in the world are you doing here?" Willard asked as Helen walked over to pour herself a cup of coffee. She sat down at the table and proceeded to tell them what had happened last evening.

"Helen, do you think his mother got to him some way?" Jane asked.

"I don't know, Mama. I don't know how she could, but with her, anything is possible. Oh, could I borrow a blanket? I don't have an extra blanket for that small bed?" Helen asked.

Jane Martin was shocked by what Helen was telling her. She went into the linen closet in her hallway and got a heavy blanket for Helen. She also got a set of single bed sheets to give her. They would still be a little big for the bed, but they would be better than a folded-up double sheet.

"Here are some sheets and an additional pillow for you along with the warmer blanket. Hopefully, you won't need them for long. David must be hurting also," Jane said to Helen.

When Helen got back to the house, David was still not awake and out of the bedroom. She took the sheets and blanket into the spare room and made up the bed, then went into the bathroom to shower and get ready for the day.

While she was in the shower, David banged on the door, yelling at her to finish up quickly, that he needed to get into the bathroom.

Helen put her dressing gown on and opened the door, saying, "You used to come into the bathroom when I was in there. What's wrong with that now? Why the banging and yelling?"

"Just hurry and get out, Helen. I need some time in there. I could use breakfast when I'm done also. A cup of coffee would be nice too," David said sarcastically.

"David, I am your wife, not your servant. I will take care of fixing your meals while you are unable to, but I would appreciate you not ordering me around. I am not one of your crew," Helen informed him. With that, she walked past his wheelchair and into the spare bedroom to get dressed.

By the time David was finished in the bathroom, dressed, and came into the kitchen in his wheelchair, Helen had his breakfast on the table with a cup of steaming hot coffee beside his plate.

"You have a 10:30 therapy appointment over at Barnes this morning. We will need to leave about 9:45 in order to avoid some of the traffic. It can get heavy going across the bridge sometimes," Helen informed David.

Helen took her crocheting with her when she took David to therapy. Mrs. Bremer had explained to her what she was doing wrong and why her dishcloth was so crooked. She needed to concentrate on what she was doing and count her stitches.

"What's that you're taking with you?" David asked as he maneuvered into the car and Helen put the wheelchair in the back.

"I am learning to crochet. I told you, I go to the Methodist church women's group every Wednesday evening. They are teaching me to crochet. It gives me something to do while I wait for you to finish therapy," Helen explained.

"And what am I supposed to do on Wednesday while you are out gossiping with the women at the church?" David asked.

"First of all, we are not gossiping. It is also a Bible study group. We are just crocheting while we are studying the Bible. Second, you should be able to take care of yourself for an hour. I will have supper all ready for you before I leave," Helen explained.

"Well, I don't like it. I want you here in the evening," said David. "David, I am not giving up my Wednesday evenings. That is my time. You are being waited on hand and foot most of the time. Please give me my one hour a week," Helen asserted. She followed David as he wheeled himself into the therapy room to make sure he was okay, then she went to the waiting room. The room was full of women and children waiting for their husbands to finish therapy. Helen was surprised at the number of women there.

She sat down in a chair a little away from the other women, pulled out her crocheting, and started working on her washcloth. She had pulled out most of her previous work and was now concentrating on keeping the rows straight. She was pretty happy with her work and was anxious to show it to Mrs. Bremer on Wednesday evening.

As she was sitting there, a tall, very pretty woman sat down beside her. "Is your husband in therapy?" she asked Helen.

"Yes, he is. This is his first appointment since he has been home," Helen answered her.

"I am Bernice Holt. My husband is Bruce Holt. He lost his right leg at Tarawa and is learning to use an artificial leg. It is not easy for him," she explained to Helen.

"I am Helen Cunningham. My husband David injured his leg when a torpedo hit his ship. After it was injured initially, he fell and broke it, causing some more severe damage. He is learning to walk on it again and doing strengthening exercises. This is his first appointment since he has been home," Helen explained.

"It is strange having him home again. Our whole house has had to be modified to accommodate his needs. It is hard for me to get used to his needs. My whole life revolves around taking care of Bruce now. I have no private time at all. He wants me around all of the time to fetch and carry for him," Bernice rambled on.

Helen continued to crochet while Bernice talked. She surmised that Bernice had no other female to talk to.

She was still rambling on when David came out of the therapy room and announced it was time to leave. Helen gathered up her crocheting, rose, and was ready to leave when Bernice grabbed her arm and said, "See you next time, Helen. It was good talking to you."

"Who was that woman you were talking to in there?" David asked as Helen was helping him into the car.

"I have no idea. She introduced herself as Bernice. Her husband was in the therapy room. He has apparently lost his leg and is learning to use a prosthesis," Helen answered David.

"Well, be careful what you say to people in there. Rumors spread like wildfires in a place like that," David said.

Helen looked at David with amazement. What did he think that she would tell some stranger all of their secrets? She didn't think they had any secrets. David's attitude towards her had changed once he wheeled himself into the house. Did he not like it? Was he upset that she had decorated it without his input as to colors, etc.? Why had he changed from a loving, caring husband over the phone to a cold, calculating one in person? She couldn't figure out why he had changed overnight.

Overnight! He obviously didn't want to sleep with her. Had she changed that much that he wasn't physically attracted to her anymore? Had he found someone else while he was away, maybe at one of the ports where they docked? She knew that he had shore leave at some of the ports. He was not confined to the ship the entire four years he was gone. She would try to talk to him when they got home.

Chapter 16

*D*avid went straight to the bedroom when they returned from the therapy appointment.

"Would you like some lunch?" Helen asked him as he was going down the hall.

"I'll tell you when I want something to eat," David answered back and closed the door to the bedroom. He came back out in a few minutes, wheeled into the bathroom, came back out in a few minutes, and wheeled back into the bedroom, closing the door behind him, all without saying another word to her.

Helen had put her crochet bag down beside the sofa, put her handbag and coat in the front closet, and went into the kitchen for a glass of water. She desperately needed someone to talk to. She didn't know what to do about David's attitude towards her and was afraid to talk to him. He was not listening to anything she had to say. He was just giving her sharp answers to her questions and pretty much ignoring her the rest of the time. At least he hadn't said anything yet today about the checkbook. She was reluctant to turn any of the finances over to him. She didn't think he was capable of handling them right now.

After leaving a sandwich and glass of milk in the refrigerator for David when he got up, Helen put an old sweater on and her garden gloves and went out to rake some leaves and clean up the last of the flower beds.

She spent about an hour working in the yard, and when she went back inside, she heard David on the phone. She was curious as to who he was talking to and was shocked to hear him talking to his mother.

"Yes, Mother. I understand that, but I have to stay here. Helen and I are married. Yes, Mother, she is feeding me. Yes, Mother, I am warm enough at night. No, Mother, I will not come and live at your house. I am still in the Navy, and my address of record is where I am now. No, Mother, do not come over here. You have done enough damage to my home and my wife. I will see you when I see you. I have enough to deal with now without having to worry about you. Good-bye, Mother," David said as he hung up the phone.

"Are you okay?" asked Helen.

"Yes! I'm okay. She is just bugging me to move into her house so she can take care of me, as she says, properly," David answered. "Thanks for the sandwich. It was good. What were you doing outside?"

"I was raking up some of the leaves and cleaning up some of the flowerbeds. In the spring, I want to plant some more flowers. The beds are pretty bare right now. The outside of the place wasn't very well taken care of. The inside just needed paint, and we will probably have to paint the outside within a couple of years," Helen explained. "Do you really like this house, David? I signed the rent-to-own agreement with a prayer that it would be okay with you. When the landlord refused to do the necessary upgrades for your wheelchair, I was kind of desperate to find someplace. I was afraid you would have to go live with your parents, and I knew that I would not be welcome there."

"I do like it. It is homey feeling, and I like the idea of owning our own home someday. It will be a lot better when I get out of this damn wheelchair. Helen, would you mind if I came to church with you on Sunday morning?" David asked.

"Of course not! I would love to have you come. The people that attend that church are so nice. They always greet me with smiles and handshakes, and a couple of the women even give me hugs, and they always ask about you and how you are. It would be so nice to introduce you to them," Helen answered with a big smile on her face.

"You know, Helen, this is not easy for me. Coming home to find that you have managed to hold a full-time job and live your life without me is hard on the ego. You handled all of the things that I used to do and apparently did a very good job of it. Nothing at all seems to be amiss. It is hard to accept that you got along so well without me," David said.

"Do you think it was easy for me?" Helen shouted at him. "Well, Mister, it was not! I was scared to death. Daddy had to show me how to write a check and how to make a deposit at the bank and how to turn the power back on when it went out in a storm. I had to learn how to fill the car with gasoline when I could get it, and I had to figure out how to use the damn ration stamps so I could eat. Along with all of that, I had to learn a new and different job, knowing all along that it was only temporary. I went to work on a Friday and was told not to come back on Monday. Now, I am scared all over again because you are home, and I have nothing to do except sit and crochet while you are in therapy. I can't even sleep in my own bed," she yelled. "You won't look at me or even touch my hand. You want to take everything away from me, including your comfort and affection. The damn war really screwed up a lot of lives, including ours."

Helen stomped off into the spare bedroom, closed the door, and sat on the cot and cried her eyes out. It was the first time she had ever yelled at David, and she felt terrible for doing it, but felt good to get it all out in the open.

David was stunned by Helen's outburst. He had no idea what she had gone through with him gone. He assumed that she would take care of everything until he got home and then he would take over again.

He rolled his chair to the spare bedroom door and knocked. "Can I come in, Helen?" he asked.

She was quiet for a minute, not answering until she composed herself.

"Please. I want to talk to you," David pleaded.

"Okay," she said as she got up and opened the door. "There is not enough room in here for your chair," Helen said as she went out of the spare room and back into the living room. David followed her and watched her sit down in the side chair next to the sofa. He moved himself onto one end of the sofa in hopes that she would sit beside him, but she made no attempt to move.

"What do you want, David, to give me some more orders?" she asked sarcastically.

"No. I want to explain my actions of the other night," he said. Helen looked at him with a grimace on her face. His actions still stung and would for a long time.

"I'm afraid too, Helen. I am afraid you won't want to touch me again. My leg is pretty mangled up, and I will have an ugly scar for the rest of my life. It will not be pretty to look at. I am not sure if I can make love to you or not. The doctors said that they are not sure if that part of me was damaged or not. The injury to my leg was very close to my private parts. There were cuts and bruises over that part of my body as well as my leg. I figured if I kept you at a distance, it would be easier on both of us," David explained.

"Do you really think that little of me that the way your leg looked would make a difference in how I felt about you? When we stood before the judge and got married six years ago, we said 'in sickness and in health, for better or worse, 'til death do us part.' I meant it when I said 'I do!' I thought you did too."

"I meant it with all my heart, but I wanted to give you an out if you wanted one. Four years is a long time to be apart. I have wanted you desperately every one of those 1,460 days. I want to have babies with you and raise those babies here in Portland with our families around us. At this point, I am not sure about my family, but that can be figured out later. I just don't know whether we can have those babies or not."

"Sweetheart, if we can't have them naturally, then we can always adopt children. We will figure it out. I love you, and I want our lives to be as normal as possible, but me sleeping on that horrible cot in the spare room is not normal. Can I please move back into the bedroom?" Helen asked with a smile on her face. She moved to sit beside him on the sofa, took his hand, and put it on her cheek. She bent over and gave him a kiss, probably the best one since he had been home. David enveloped her in his arms and cried like a baby out of relief that she still loved him and wanted him.

"It will take me a while, Helen, to be able to expose my leg to you. I have to get used to it myself. I want to get strong enough that I can stand on my own and walk without this wheelchair. That should take about a month, the therapist says, if I work really hard. Can you wait that long?" David asked.

"If that is what you want, I will wait. I just want to know that you are getting better and still want me as your wife," Helen answered.

Helen got up and turned on the radio to listen to the news. Most of the national news was taken up with the information on the plans for the war crimes trials to be held in Nuremberg, Germany. The Allies had managed to arrest and detain many of the high-ranking Nazis and were putting them on trial. The presiding judge would be an American, along with the prosecuting attorney. Helen was tired of listening to war news. She had had almost five years of it by now, but David wanted to know what was going on and wanted to listen to the news all of the time.

"Could we please turn the radio off while we eat, David, or at least turn it to some music instead of the news?" she asked.

"I would prefer to hear the news," David said as a matter of course. "We didn't get much news about the European War while we were at sea. I need to catch up."

Helen decided that an argument was not worth the effort and ignored the radio. She had put dinner on the table for them, but David said he was not hungry and continued to sit on the sofa listening to the news. Obviously, things were not completely cleared up between them. David continued to take Helen for granted and assumed that she would do exactly as he asked and expected. She would like to have been able to go to a counselor of some kind but was afraid to bring it up to David. She was sure he would not approve and would not even consider going.

Helen was hoping that after their talk the night before, things would ease up between them, but it didn't appear that they were going to. David still continued to issue orders and expect them to be carried out immediately. He still did not want her in the bedroom with him, so she slept in the spare room again last night.

Helen missed the Wednesday evening meeting at church the night before. She looked forward to those times with the ladies, but she couldn't leave David after the talk that they had had. On reflection, she probably would have been better off going to the meeting. On Thursday morning, he was in a foul mood. He had a 10:30 therapy appointment that morning and was not very kind to her as she was trying to get ready to go. He hardly gave her time to use the bathroom before they left. Then he criticized her driving all the way over to Vancouver and the hospital. She was so nervous by the time they got there that she was almost in tears.

"I am going to wait for you in the car. You can get yourself into the building," Helen announced.

"I can't open the door and wheel myself in at the same time. You have to come in to help me," David barked at her.

"Wait for someone to come along to help you. I am not getting out of this car until we get back home. I will come around and get your chair for you, but that is all. You need to learn to do things for yourself. I'm tired!" Helen said.

"We'll talk about this later," David growled.

He got out of the car, and just as he was wheeling up to the door, an orderly came along and held the door open for him.

Helen breathed a sigh of relief when he was out of the car. She was so pent up and so angry at him and did not want to listen to Bernice's constant chatter for an hour. What was she going to do? She knew that Gloria and Marian were going through the same problems with Josh and Michael, but they had the kids to be concerned about too.

The kids hardly knew their fathers and were not used to them issuing the orders and doing the disciplining. Mama always did it, and now it was Daddy. He was a lot stricter than Mama. All of them were normally good students, but their grades had started falling when their dads got home. Both Gloria and Marian had had conferences with their teachers. This seemed to be a common problem in families with dads returning from war.

Halloween was coming up in a couple of weeks, and Helen was thinking she would get a couple of pumpkins, carve them, and put them on the front porch to attract the trick-or-treaters. She didn't know how many kids they would get at this place. They didn't get a lot at the apartment, but it was fun seeing them all dressed up in their costumes.

When she mentioned the idea to David on the way home, he said absolutely not. He did not want a bunch of kids running up and down the ramp and ringing their doorbell. He said it was just a waste of money buying pumpkins that were going to rot in a couple of days anyway.

Nothing Helen could say or do seemed to please David. She had hoped that he would be more open once they had talked the other night, but he was even worse than before.

"Do you want to go to church with me on Sunday morning before we go to my parents for dinner? You had said you would like to go," Helen asked him.

"I've changed my mind. I really don't want to go, and I would prefer you not go either. It is just a bunch of gibberish that they talk about anyway. And as far as Wednesday nights are concerned, I need you at home with me, so I don't want you going to that ladies' gab session," David announced.

"You are not taking church away from me, David. I will go to church on Sunday mornings, and I will go to my parents for dinner on Sunday afternoon. I will also go to the Wednesday Bible study. You have taken everything else away; you are not taking that."

"Then don't expect me to be here when you get back," he said.

"And where do you think you will be?" she asked.

"I will be at my parents!" David stated.

Helen did not say a word for a few minutes, then said, "Maybe that would be the best place for you right now. Let your mother and father put up with your garbage. I am tired of it."

When she pulled into the driveway, Helen got out, got the wheelchair out for David, and put it beside his open passenger door. Then she left and went into the house, went to the spare room, closed the door, and this time was so mad she couldn't cry. She figured she was pretty much cried out.

Today was Thursday, the 25th. She had to live through Friday and Saturday before she could go to church on Sunday and then to her parents' home.

David was in the living room yelling at her to get out of the bedroom and fix him some lunch. She ignored the noise and took out her crocheting and began to work on her dishcloth. She could hear David coming down the hallway hollering that he was hungry. He pounded on the door, but she ignored him. Finally, after a few more pounds on the door, she told him there was food in the refrigerator; he could fix his own lunch.

"I can't fix my own meals sitting in this chair?" he hollered through the closed door.

"You can if you are hungry enough," was all Helen said to him.

All was quiet for a while except for the rattle of pots and pans in the kitchen. She had no idea what he was fixing for himself, and she really didn't care. She had put together a meatloaf earlier in the morning and would fix that for dinner tonight, but she was not going to go out of her way to accommodate her husband right now.

Chapter 17

Helen's life right now consisted of taking David to therapy appointments three times a week, fixing him breakfast and dinner, and going to Bible study on Wednesday at 6:00 o'clock and church on Sunday at 11:00 AM. She went to her parents' home after church for dinner with the family, but David refused to go. He said he did not want the confusion of the kids running around the house. Helen had told him about Willard's camping trips with them and how much better behaved they were now, but he didn't believe her.

"They are probably worse now since their dads have not been there. They ran wild before. Now they are probably delinquents. I don't want to be around them if they are like that," David stated firmly.

"Your loss, David. My family would like to see you. You haven't even made an effort to see my sisters since you have been home," Helen said.

"I can't stand the constant chatter. You go ahead and go. I will stay here and make do for myself," David said with a pout on his face. "Just make sure there is something for me to eat before you leave."

"Fix it yourself!" Helen hollered at him as she went into the bathroom to get ready for church.

The message at church that morning was about forgiveness, but Helen was not really listening. She was so confused about David's attitude. The other day, he said that he might go to his parents' house, but he had not followed through with that. She was afraid to ask him why. She knew that his mother would come and pick him up at the drop of a hat if he took the least bit of interest in moving in with them. He seemed to want to stay and torture her for some reason.

Helen drove from church to her parents' home. Apparently, she was the only one who would be there for dinner. Her sisters and their families were visiting in-laws for the day.

Jane had fixed a simple meal of fried chicken, mashed potatoes and gravy, and candied carrots for dinner. It was one of David's favorite meals and Jane was hoping that he would be there, but she realized that he was not when Helen came in the back door right into the kitchen.

"I'm sorry David is not with you, honey. Are things getting any better for the two of you?" Jane asked her daughter.

"No, they are not! I think they are probably getting worse. He wants me to stop going to Bible study on Wednesday evenings and doesn't want me to go to church on Sunday. He says it's just a bunch of garbage that they preach and I should not believe a word they are saying. Mama, the war has really changed him. I know he was not raised in a religious family. Neither was I, but we always believed in a higher power. We never turned our noses up at religion and I didn't ever hear David say anything bad about other people believing in a specific religion. But he does now. He berates people for attending church. He told me that they had church services on the ship on Sunday mornings, then would fire the big guns and kill other human beings. He says he hated the Japanese for what they did at Pearl Harbor and for continuing to kill Americans, but he doesn't understand a God that would allow one race of people to do that to another. He compares it to what the Germans did to the Jews," Helen explained to her mother.

"Have you thought about getting another job? I am sure there is something out there that you would be able to do," Jane asked.

"I wish I could. It would give me something to do during the day, but I have to be available to take David to his therapy appointments and I do need to fix meals for him. I really don't think he should be trying to use the stove while he is in the wheelchair. The controls are on the back of the stove and he would have to reach over a hot burner to turn it off. He is on his own for lunch, though. He is perfectly capable of getting what he needs out of the refrigerator and the cupboards. I have moved the dishes and glassware to the lower cupboards so he can reach them. He doesn't like it, but I pretty much ignore his protests now," Helen said.

"Have you suggested some counseling with him? That might help," Jane asked.

"At this point, Mama, I wouldn't even ask. He would be furious with me for even suggesting the idea. I am thinking of talking to Reverend Corbin, though. He is the only one I can think of who will listen to my needs and not talk about what David needs to assimilate back into civilian life. I am really tired of my needs being ignored in favor of the returning warriors," Helen said sarcastically.

Helen got home late that afternoon with a plate of food for David only to find the kitchen a mess. There were dirty pots and pans on the stove, the sink was piled with dirty dishes, and food was spilled all over the floor.

"What in the hell happened in here?" Helen yelled. "It looks like a hurricane came through the kitchen."

"If you would have stayed home and fixed me a meal like you are supposed to, this would not have happened," David said. "Don't blame me!" he yelled back from the living room where he was listening to the news of the war crime trials in Germany.

Helen stormed into the living room and said, "I left everything in the refrigerator for you to fix yourself a sandwich for lunch and told you I would fix you supper when I got home. What in the world were you trying to fix?" she asked.

"There was some kind of a piece of meat in there and I was going to try to fix that. I wanted some potatoes, but I couldn't find them. I got mad and started pulling things out of the cupboards. Because of your negligence, the kitchen is a mess and I am hungry," David announced to his wife.

"I have brought a plate of food for you from Mother. It is one of your favorites. Go ahead and eat it, then you can start on cleaning up the kitchen. I am not going to do it. You made the mess; you clean it up," Helen said as she walked out of the kitchen, down the hall, and into the spare room, which apparently now was her bedroom for what seemed to be the long run. There was no sign that he wanted her back with him and she probably wouldn't go now if he asked her. There had to be a lot of changes before she would even consider getting back into bed with him.

Helen heard a lot of rattling and banging of pots and pans coming from the kitchen and water running in the sink. David was tall enough to reach up and over the edge of the sink, so he was able to wash the dishes. There was a mop in the broom closet, so he was going to have to figure out how to use it to clean the floor. Otherwise, he would track food on the wheels of his chair onto the carpet in the living room.

She knew that she would be up very early in the morning mopping the floor again, but he would have to do the initial cleanup.

David had a therapy appointment on Monday morning at 10 AM. David usually rested after the appointment for a while before he ate lunch. While he was resting, she was going to call Rev. Corbin and make an appointment to see him on Wednesday before Bible study. She would tell David that she had to be there early to help set up. The lady who usually did it was out of town.

The drive over to David's therapy appointment on Wednesday was very stressful. There had been an accident on the bridge that held up traffic for a short time and David did nothing but criticize Helen's driving and yell at the other drivers to get out of the way. By the time they arrived at the parking lot, Helen was a nervous wreck and almost in tears. Again, she got David's chair out of the trunk of the car for him, but didn't go in with him. She needed to sit and relax and not listen to the other women chatting as if they didn't have a care in the world.

David's workout was hard that day and he wasn't in a much better mood going home than he was getting there. The traffic was better, but apparently, according to David, Helen's driving wasn't. She didn't drive fast enough or her hand signals were not clear enough, or she was too close to the car in front of her, or she was too far away from the car in front of her. She didn't pass cars when she had a chance and she was a timid driver. She did nothing right, according to David.

When she told David that she had to be at church at five o'clock instead of six, he was furious with her and told her she couldn't go.

"I will be there at five o'clock, David. I have promised that I would be there to help and I will be. You will have your hot supper on the table before I leave, so don't worry. You will get fed. I don't want a repeat of what happened in the kitchen on Sunday. You broke two of my good dishes. I don't want to lose any more. Don't ever try to stop me from going to my Bible study classes or going to church on Sunday, or for that matter going to my parents' house for dinner. Those are things I will not give up."

Helen was not sure what would happen over the holidays. Obviously, she would not be invited to his parents' home. Before the war, they alternated holidays with their families.

This year, she was not sure what David would want to do. He might just go to his parents' home without her.

Just as soon as Thanksgiving was over, she would go to the basement and get the two boxes of Christmas decorations that they had and start putting them up. Hopefully, they could get a tree the next weekend. She was anxious to decorate this year. While David was gone, she didn't have a tree. She put up a few decorations and always had a wreath for the door, but that was about all. This year, she wanted to go all out and use all of their holiday décor.

But when she told David her plans, he objected to the decorations and a tree. He felt that a tree would be too messy inside the house and would be a waste of money. It would just die and they would have to throw it away right after Christmas.

"But David, we always had a Christmas tree!" Helen said in an astounded voice.

"Well, not this year. I don't want the mess in the house," he announced.

"What's the difference? You don't clean it up anyway," Helen shot back at him as she stormed out the kitchen door. As the wind hit her, she realized she did not have her coat on, but wasn't about ready to go back inside and get it. She paced the carport back and forth until she was so cold she had to go back inside. When she went back in, she heard the news on the radio again. It seemed like it was never off when David was in there.

Helen went to the kitchen. She put a potato in the oven to bake and took out the leftover meatloaf to heat when the potato was almost done. Along with a green salad, she felt that would be a good dinner for David. She set the table and had everything ready to put the food on just before she left.

Just before she was ready to leave for church, Helen got the potato and meatloaf out of the oven, put it on a plate with the salad. She had some dressing for the salad on the table along with butter for the potato and ketchup for the meatloaf. She had made him a cup of coffee and had a glass of water ready for him.

When Helen went into the living room, she informed David that dinner was on the table for him, that she was leaving for church now.

"I'm not hungry now. Save it for later," he informed her.

"Either you eat it now, or you eat it later cold. That's your choice. I am leaving for church," Helen announced and left the house through the front door.

Helen had gotten in the habit of having her handbag and the keys to the car with her most of the time. When she was home, they were in the spare bedroom with her things. David could not wheel himself into that room. The doorway was too narrow for his chair, so she knew that for the time being, her things were safe in there. She was terrified that he would take the keys to the car away from her. She decided that the next time she had to go grocery shopping, she would stop at the hardware store and have another key made. Helen wasn't at all sure that he wouldn't try to get behind the wheel and drive. She didn't think that he could move his foot fast enough from the accelerator to the brake while using the clutch with his other foot.

Chapter 18

Helen was very nervous when she walked into Rev. Corbin's office on Wednesday evening. She had never talked to anyone except her parents and sisters about her personal life, and this would not be easy for her, but she had to get some of this frustration out and figure out what to do about David and her marriage. She didn't want to lose either one of them.

Helen was not the first young wife of a returning serviceman who had come to him for advice. He had not realized how widespread the problem was for the women who were left behind during the war. It was eye-opening to him to hear the stories of frustration, fear, and abuse coming from these women who had put their lives on hold for so many years in order to serve their country here at home.

Rev. Corbin started the conversation with a few questions about Helen's background and where she grew up, then proceeded to ask her about David and their lives together. As Helen began talking to him, she opened up a little more and explained to the pastor about what was happening with David right now and the way he was treating her. She explained that she was frustrated and did not know what to do. She wanted to maintain her marriage but also wanted some respect from David and acknowledgment of what she went through while he was gone.

"Will David come to church with you, Helen?" the Reverend asked.

"He indicated once that he would like to come, but when I suggested it on Saturday evening, he said he had changed his mind and didn't even want me to come. He doesn't want me to come to Bible study on Wednesdays either," she explained.

"Helen, has he harmed you in any way since he has been home? Physically, I mean," Rev. Corbin asked quietly.

"No. He acted like he wanted to a couple of times, but he can't get out of his chair right now without great effort and I have been staying clear of him," Helen said.

"Good. Be sure to protect yourself. Does David drive the car?"

"No, not yet, but he has expressed the desire to do so. He thinks that in a few weeks, he will be able to move his foot from the accelerator to the brake fast enough to be safe in driving. I have not given him the keys yet, although he has asked for them. I am going to have another key made so that I will not be without one," Helen explained.

"Helen, I will tell you that you are not the first young woman who has come to me for advice with the same problem, and you probably won't be the last. I certainly do not have all the answers, but I can tell you, as I have told the other ladies, take care of yourself, physically and mentally. Try to stay calm during the confrontations. Look out for your own safety. Be aware of what is going on around you. Are there any other influences in your husband's life that could affect his relationship with you? I hate to mention it, but could there be another woman in his life that you are not aware of? Just be very careful of your feelings. I know it is very hard to do when you are being yelled at and criticized all of the time, but be aware. You are a good person and deserve to have the best possible surroundings," Rev. Corbin said.

"I want to let you know that I am going to write a sermon touching on the subject of what women are going through right now with their husbands home and taking over the household again," he was explaining to Helen.

"Oh no, Rev. Corbin. I don't want anyone to know that I have spoken to you or that there is trouble in my marriage," Helen cried out.

"I would never mention any names, Helen, or expose you or any of the ladies I have talked to in any way. What you say to me in confidence stays that way. Nothing is written down or recorded in any way. Please be assured of that. I just think it is necessary for the congregation to understand what the women who stayed behind did for the country and what you had to sacrifice to do it," he reassured her. "It is necessary for them to realize the emotions that all of the women are going through now with their husbands home."

Helen looked at her watch and said, "Thank you, Rev. Corbin, for talking to me. I feel much better. You are the first person I have talked to besides my mother, who has been concerned about me and my feelings. I appreciate it. I had best get to Bible study. I don't want to be late." She shook Rev. Corbin's hand and went down the hallway to the Bible study room, feeling much better about herself and her prospects.

She learned to finish off her dishcloth that evening and started another. Her first effort was a little crooked, but she was satisfied with her first crochet project. She was going to have to go to Woolworth's and get some different colored yarn. Maybe she could get some red or green and make a dishcloth for her mother for Christmas. That would be fun.

When Helen arrived home that evening, David was sitting in his chair in front of the door when she walked in. She looked at him and asked what he was doing.

"I have packed an overnight bag. I am going to my parents' home for a few days. Dad is coming to get me in a few minutes.

We need some time apart. You are not listening to me or doing what I need you to do for me. You need a few days to think about our future and even if you want a future with me," David said.

"Go! Go back to your mama. Let her fawn over you and take care of you like you were a little boy. Let her say nasty things about me so that you will think it is my fault that you got hurt during the war. Go! At this point, I don't care," Helen cried as she ran to the spare bedroom, slammed the door, and cried her heart out.

She heard the doorbell ring about 10 minutes later, heard David greet his father, and roll his chair down the ramp. Then she heard the car drive away from the house.

She slowly walked out of the spare bedroom, into the living room, and then into the kitchen to call her mother and father and let them know what happened. They offered to come over, but she refused, saying that she needed to be alone that evening. She would see them the next day.

When she hung up, she went around and made sure all of the doors were locked and bolted and all of the windows shut and locked. She did not want David or his mother or father coming back that evening.

After fixing herself a cup of tea, Helen went into the bedroom, stripped the bed of the dirty sheets, and put clean ones on. Then she moved all of her things back into the main bedroom and put them neatly back into her dresser drawers and the closet. After she finished doing that, she went into the bathroom and took a nice hot bath, dressed in a fresh nightgown, and climbed into her bed for the first time in weeks. And for the first time since David had been home, she had a good night's sleep.

On Thursday, she did not hear from David at all and she did not try to contact him. He had a therapy appointment on Friday, but she assumed his father would take him. She would not. Her parents wanted to come over, but she asked them not to. She needed the alone time to try and figure things out. All kinds of things were going through her head. She would probably have to look for a job. She would need the income if David cut her off. She really wanted to keep this house but didn't know how she could do it without his income, and by rights, the money she had saved was David's money, so she would have no claim on it.

She stepped out onto the porch in the morning to get the newspaper. She looked around, but nothing seemed to be amiss in the yard or the neighborhood. She bolted the door when she went back inside and sat at the kitchen table with her coffee and the employment section of the paper in front of her. She was reading through the want ads, not finding any real opportunities for women in the workforce when she happened to see an ad for an "Inventory Control Clerk" at Sears, Roebuck and Company. She looked again and noticed that the ad was under the heading of men wanted, but with the experience she had at Continental Can and the fact that she had worked at Sears before, maybe she would qualify.

Dressed in her best business suit and with the ad in hand, she drove to Sears on Grand Avenue, about four miles from her home. She walked up to the personnel office and found that the same lady who worked there five years before was still there.

"Well, hello, Helen. How are you? It has been a long time since we have seen you in here. What can I do for you?" Edith Carpenter asked.

"I am here to apply for the job of inventory clerk," Helen stated and pointed out the ad in the newspaper she had with her.

"Helen, that job is for a man, not a woman," Edith said.

"Has anyone applied? I have four and a half years' experience as an inventory control clerk with Continental Can Company. My former boss there, Marvin Swenson, will give me a good reference. I think that I can do a good job for you."

"We really were expecting a man to apply for the job, but none has so far and it has been advertised for four days now. Let me talk to Mr. Jacobs, the personnel manager, about this and see if he will speak to you. Please have a seat in the waiting area and I will get back to you," Edith said.

About 15 minutes later, Edith came out of Mr. Jacobs' office and asked Helen to step in, that Mr. Jacobs would see her now.

"Hello, Helen. I remember you working here about five years ago in the handbag and millinery department. I understand from Edith that you worked at Continental Can during the war," Mr. Jacobs inquired.

"Yes, I worked in the inventory control department, coordinating the buying of the materials, the manufacture of the cans, and the distribution to the plants where they were packed with food for the military overseas. It was a taxing job and took a lot of concentration, but I enjoyed the challenge," Helen explained.

"Yes, I just spoke with Mr. Swenson about you. He said you were one of the best workers that he had ever had and that I should hire you on the spot. The problem is, the job is posted for a man and I have to leave it open for at least 10 days to see if a qualified man applies. If one does, I am obligated to hire him first, but if we have no applicants within that ten-day period, the job is yours. Can you wait that long?" he asked. "Yes. Certainly, I can. My husband is staying with his parents now and I am not sure when he will be home, so I am free and able to start anytime you want," Helen explained.

After a few more minutes of conversation, Mr. Jacobs got up, shook Helen's hand, and told her he would get in touch with her in 10 days, even if she did not get the job.

"Thank you very much, Mr. Jacobs. I look forward to hearing from you," Helen said as she left the office. She waved to Edith as she walked out.

When she got into the car, she started to shake. What had she done? She would know in 10 days if she had the job. She applied for the job without telling anyone what she was doing. What would David say? This might be the catalyst that will make him leave for good. She didn't want to lose David or her marriage, but she had to do something to save her sanity. She wanted so much to be a partner in this marriage, but David wouldn't listen right now.

She drove home with some trepidation, wondering if David would be there. He did have a key to the house, so he could get in. She didn't want either Roger or Alice in the house without her there. She was afraid Alice would do some damage.

As she pulled into the driveway, she noticed that everything seemed to be the same as it was except the mailman had been there and a package was sitting on the porch. Obviously, David had not been there or he would have taken the mail and package in.

She pulled the mail out of the box, opened the door, and placed the mail and her handbag on the table beside the door, then went back out to pick up the package. She looked at it carefully when she got it in and realized it was not sent through the mail. There was no postage or return address on the box.

Helen carefully opened the box. It was about 20 inches long and 12 inches wide and only about 3 inches deep; an odd size box. She opened the lid and found a scrub board in the box. It was not very large and was just a plain wood and metal scrub board. Who in the world would send her a scrub board?

In the bottom of the box, she found a note.

"I have won!" the note said. "You can't even wash his clothes. You have to take them to your mama's house. I will take care of him the way he should be taken care of. I will feed him, make sure he is tucked in at night, and make sure he has a proper bath. I won!"

The note was signed, "Alice Cunningham."

A scrub board! What in the hell was she thinking? What is wrong with taking our clothes to my mother's house to use the washing machine? She has really gone off her rocker this time.

Helen went to the phone and called the Cunningham house to talk to David.

"Let me talk to David," she said when the phone was answered.

"Never. He is mine now and you will not hurt him anymore." The receiver was slammed down in her ear.

She sat down in the chair at the kitchen table and looked at the scrub board. Maybe she could use it as a decoration in the kitchen. Then she looked through the mail. There were two pretty important letters for David. They had Department of the Navy return addresses on them.

She called the Cunningham house again. This time Roger answered the phone. Helen explained about the letters and that she had to get them to David. "Roger, please let me see David. We will not be able to solve anything if she doesn't let me talk to him,"

"Helen, she is adamant about you not seeing him. She is acting like he is a small boy again. I am not sure what to do.

So far, David is putting up with her actions, but that won't last for long. She says that she is going to give him his bath tonight before she tucks him into bed. There is nothing that I can do!" Roger said meekly.

"Be a man, Roger. Stop her or tell David to stop her. She is living in a fantasy world and has to wake up," Helen said as she put the receiver down.

Chapter 19

Helen opened the two letters that were addressed to David. The letters had to do with his discharge from the Navy. He needed to have the information, so she decided to drive over to the Cunningham house and leave the letters on the porch. She put the letters in a larger envelope and wrote "DAVID" on the outside. She added the phrase, "Personal and Confidential" under his name. She would leave the letters and hope that he got them.

Helen walked up onto the porch at the Cunningham house, left the letters in front of the door, rang the doorbell, and walked back to her car. As she got into the car, she saw Roger Cunningham open the door, pick up the letter, and look right at her. He gave her a nod and went back into the house, closing the door behind him.

With Roger getting the letters, she was pretty sure that David would get them. According to the letters, David was due to be discharged from the Navy, and he would receive some kind of a medal for his service. She wished that she could be at the ceremony when they presented him with the medal, but she doubted whether she would be able to go.

Helen felt downhearted when she reached the house. She was sad that the house was empty again. It was like when David was away. She just felt empty inside, but this time was different.

David was home, but not in their home, and he was drastically changed.

Helen called her mother to let her know about the possible job that she could have with Sears. She also told her about the two letters that she delivered to the Cunningham home.

"I really don't know what to do about all of this, Mama," Helen said. "My life is really a mess now. I applied for that job on the spur of the moment because I thought David might cut me off financially. What do I do if I get the job and David wants to come back home? He will be furious with me, but I want to work. I need to work for my own well-being. I have been working for six years, four of them without David around. Doing a good job gave me a sense of self-worth."

"Go ahead and take the job if it is offered to you. It will be a good job for you and give you some self-satisfaction. If David does decide to come home, he will just have to learn to live with you working. I am assuming that he will eventually go back to work," Jane said.

"He wants to as soon as the doctor will release him and as soon as he is separated from the Navy. He is not sure if he will be strong enough to do the work in the shipyard that he did before the war, but there should be something there that he will be qualified for," Helen explained.

"Helen, have you ever thought of having a private talk with David's doctor? He might be able to explain to you what is going on with David," Jane asked.

"Do you think he would talk to me? Information between a doctor and patient is always confidential," Helen responded.

"He might not be able to talk to you specifically about David unless David has given him permission to, but he might be able to give you some insight as to the general problem with men returning from war and how they feel about being injured. It might be worth a try?" Jane commented.

"Thanks, Mama. I will call and see if I can get an appointment with him," Helen said as she hung up the phone.

Helen looked in some of the papers that David had left and found the name of his doctor at Barnes Hospital. She called his number and made an appointment to see him on Tuesday, the 27th of November. She wanted the appointment on a day when David did not have therapy, but had to wait until after Thanksgiving to see the doctor.

Thanksgiving. She supposed she would go to her parents' home, but she wasn't very excited about it. Her Mama and Dad would be very upset if she didn't show up.

She called her mother back to let her know that she had an appointment on the 27th with David's doctor and asked what she could bring for Thanksgiving dinner.

"Just bring yourself, honey. You can help with cleanup. That will be your great contribution. I am always exhausted when one of these big dinners is over. It will seem strange without Richard, Cheryl, and Jeremy gone, but according to Cheryl's last letter, they will be having a Thanksgiving dinner in England. All of the Americans will get together and have a great, traditional turkey dinner," Jane explained.

"I will be there early, Mama, to help you with the preparation too. How would it be if I came on Wednesday and stayed the night? That way I could be of more help to you. I really will need something to do to keep my mind off of David," Helen asked.

"That would be perfect. I will look forward to having you here, honey," Jane said as she hung up the phone.

Helen was really at loose ends. She sat and crocheted for a while with the Boston Pops on the radio, but she was restless and needed something more to do. She decided to go down to the basement and go through some of her old boxes of stuff.

She pulled some boxes down from a high shelf and started going through them. She realized that one of the boxes was all the souvenirs she and David had saved from their wedding and honeymoon. She had forgotten that her wedding anniversary was coming up in two weeks. December 1, 1939, was the date they were married. What a lovely wedding they had in her parents' home. It was small but perfect. They were so much in love. Helen was only 18 years old, and David was 20, and they had such high hopes for an incredible life together. Now look at them! David was back living with his crazy mother, and she was in this lovely home she had found for them, all by herself. This was not the way it was supposed to be.

Helen lovingly packed all of those memories back in the box and returned it to the shelf. Maybe another box would be easier on her heart. But the box she chose was full of David's high school things. She closed that one right away and put it back up on the shelf.

This idea of sorting through her old things was not working out. She looked around the basement to see if there was anything else she could do to clean it up a little. She saw the empty space where a washing machine would go and all of the clotheslines her Dad had put up for her. She decided then and there that if she went to work at Sears in a couple of weeks, she would buy a new washing machine. She could make payments on it, and she would get an employee discount. Then she would not have to take her clothes over to her mother's house every week. She could wash when she wanted to. When the weather was clear in the spring and summer, she could hang the clothes outside. Finally, she had a plan!

Helen had no word from David. She tried to call him a couple of times, but was hung up on by Alice. She always seemed to answer the phone. She went to her parents' home on Wednesday evening to help her mother with Thanksgiving dinner. Her sisters and their families were there, but it was a quiet dinner. Both Gloria and Marian were having trouble adjusting to their husbands being home too. And the kids were acting like they were scared to death of their Dads. They were unusually quiet and only talked to respond to a question. When their Dads talked to them, they answered in "Yes, sir" or "No, sir" answers.

When dinner was over, the kids went into the living room to sit and read, as their father had told them to. Helen and her sisters followed their mother into the kitchen to clean up.

"Gloria, what is wrong with the girls? They hardly said a word at dinner. They are so quiet," Helen asked her sister.

"They are both afraid to say much. Josh yells at them all of the time and berates them for what they do say. Because their grades started falling when Josh came home, they now have strict reading and studying times. One of the reading times is after dinner. They have to read for an hour after dinner every evening. He has set up a schedule for them after school. Schoolwork and studying come first. They are not allowed to have any free time during the week. Usually, on Saturdays and Sundays, they have a couple of hours when they can play. It breaks my heart to see them lose their spirit, but there is not much I can do about it. He is their father and has the final say in their upbringing," Gloria explained.

Marian turned to face her sisters and said, "Same here. Maybe not quite as strict, but close to it. Only difference is, I am about ready to put a stop to it. The war screwed with Mike's mind, and he is either going to get help or the girls and I are leaving. I will not put up with his shit anymore!"

Alice was standing at the stove, putting food into storage containers with tears running down her face. Helen saw her and walked over to put an arm around her. "Oh, Mama, this is not the way it was supposed to be. We were all supposed to be happily married, and we were supposed to have a joyous and happy Thanksgiving meal together. I am so sorry that we have disappointed you and Daddy and spoiled your day."

"You three have not spoiled my day. Even your husbands have not spoiled my day, even though I don't approve of what they are doing to you or to my granddaughters. The damn war spoiled my day. Sure, we stopped the Nazis from inflicting any more horror on the world and we stopped the Japanese from taking over the rest of Asia and the Pacific, but what did we do to ourselves? We caused havoc with the minds of our loved ones. What is this world going to be like now with the threat of an atom bomb looming over us? I am afraid that we have created a world where humanity will be in fear all of the time, whether from outside forces or from inside the family," Jane lectured.

"Mama, that is the most I have heard you say in a long time," Marian said, laughing. "But you are right. The war did play havoc on all of our lives."

The ladies finished putting the food away and cleaning the kitchen when both Josh and Mike came in to say it was time for them to get home. Gloria and Marian both gave their mother and sister a hug goodbye, went into the other room, and got their coats and hats on. The granddaughters were standing quietly at the door, ready to leave. They gave their grandparents and Aunt Helen hugs and a thank you and walked out the door followed by their mothers and fathers.

Both Willard and Jane had sad looks on their faces when they left. Helen had planned to stay another night with her parents to help put the house back together again.

Helen went back to her home on Friday morning. She knew that the stores would be very busy with people doing their first big Christmas shopping, so she decided to avoid them. She did not want to deal with crowds today.

As she was driving home, she was remembering a conversation that she and David had when he was in the hospital in San Francisco. He had mentioned wanting to get a dog. That would be a good idea for her. She could get a dog for company. She decided to drive down to Columbia Blvd. to the Humane Society and see if they had any dogs available for adoption.

When she walked into the building, she could hear all of the barking from the back kennels. She asked the man at the front desk if they had any older dogs for adoption. She thought that one that was already housebroken would be better for her, especially if she was going to be working every day.

As she walked along the row of kennels, she noticed a sad looking dog in the back of a cage, just looking at her with sad eyes.

"What's his story?" Helen asked the attendant.

"He was brought in yesterday. He was found alongside the road, cold and wet and very hungry. Someone had either lost him or abandoned him. He has no collar or tag on him."

"Can I go in and pet him?" Helen asked.

"Sure. He is very gentle and not aggressive at all," the attendant answered.

Helen walked into the cage, squatted down by the door, and gently talked to the scared dog. The dog looked at her for a few seconds, got up, and slowly walked over to her and sat down right in front of her, putting his paw up like he wanted to shake hands with her. Helen laughed and took his paw and shook it. "How do you do?" she said to the dog. "I am very glad to meet you. Would you like to come home with me?"

The dog put his other paw up on her hand and gave one bark. Both Helen and the attendant laughed, and Helen stood up and said, "You, sweet dog, have a new home!"

After completing the necessary paperwork, Helen put the dog in the back seat of her car and promptly went to the grocery store.

"You stay here like a good boy, and I will go in and get you some food. I will be right back," she said to the dog.

When she came back out, the dog was sitting in the front passenger seat with his nose to the window. His tail started wagging when she came to the car and put the bag of dog food and other items needed into the trunk of the car.

When she got home, she let the dog into the house, and he promptly laid down in front of the sofa and went to sleep. He was home. Helen laughed and took the bag of food to the kitchen. She had purchased not only food but treats, a bowl for food and one for water, a mat to put the bowls on, a dog leash and collar, and a couple of toys for him to play with.

When Helen was finished putting everything away, she went in to sit on the sofa and read the newspaper. When she sat down, the dog promptly jumped up and laid down beside her with his head on her lap. "What am I going to call you?" she asked the dog. The attendant at the humane society said they had no idea what his name was and that he was probably about two years old. He was a mixed-breed dog, but mostly lab, the attendant thought. He was black with a few brown spots on his back and one on his face. Helen wanted a unique name for him. He did look very dignified when he sat in front of her, and Helen had always thought the name Stanley was a very dignified name.

"Stanley it is!" Helen said as she held his head up and looked into his eyes. "I will have a tag made with your name and phone number on it. You can wear it on your collar."

Helen called her parents to tell them about Stanley and ask her Dad if he could maybe build Stanley a doghouse for the backyard. She was going to have to install a fence back there so he could be out while she was at work.

Her mom and dad came over to Helen's house to meet Stanley and see what size doghouse Stanley would need. They fell in love with him. Willard said that he had just the right wood in his garage and would build a doghouse for him this weekend. It would give him something constructive to do so he wouldn't just sit around and eat leftovers.

The weekend was a little more tolerable with Stanley to take care of. Helen managed to keep busy taking him for a couple of walks a day and playing with him. Stanley had decided that the rug beside Helen's bed was the best place for him to sleep at night. He was very good about not getting on the bed. She really didn't want him up there, but beside the bed was good. On Sunday afternoon, when Helen returned from church, Willard brought over a large doghouse and put it in the backyard. It was even painted the soft blue color of the house and had his name over the door. Jane had an old blanket that she had washed and fixed for the inside of the doghouse so Stanley didn't have to lay on the cold plywood floor. Helen thought it was the best doghouse she had ever seen. Stanley marched right into his new home, turned around several times, and promptly laid down and closed his eyes. Helen, Willard, and Jane laughed at him, but had to take him back inside because there was no fence around the property yet.

On Monday, Helen and Stanley went to the hardware store and made arrangements for someone to come and fence in her backyard. It would cost her $75.00 to fence her whole yard. She decided to go ahead and spend the money out of her savings and have the entire backyard fenced. That way she could have a fenced-in garden in the spring and summer.

Chapter 20

On Tuesday morning, Helen dressed in her good suit, put on a hat, took Stanley with her, and drove to Barnes Hospital in Vancouver for her appointment with Captain Ronald Walker, David's doctor. She was nervous going into the appointment but was determined to get some answers as to why David was acting the way he was. He had never been that way before.

She opened the windows in the car a bit for Stanley, told him she would be back soon, and walked into the office building. As she walked into the doctor's office, she introduced herself to the receptionist and was ushered right into the office.

"Hello, Mrs. Cunningham. I am Doctor Walker. I am glad to meet you finally. David has talked about you a lot."

Helen looked at the doctor askance, saying, "Probably not very good things."

"No. He has said nothing but good things about you, as a matter of fact," the doctor corrected.

Helen sat down in the chair indicated by the doctor. She was really confused. Why was David saying good things about her when he was berating her and criticizing her at home and now not living there?

"Do you know, Doctor, that David has moved back to his parents' home?" Helen asked. "He says he doesn't approve of me going to Bible study on Wednesday evenings or going to church on Sunday. He seems to want me at his beck and call all of the time."

"I did not know that he had moved out, but I did suspect that he was not happy with the situation at home. I find this in a lot of the men coming back from battle. They are used to either giving orders or following orders. Your husband was used to giving orders to the men under his command. He was in charge of a group of men on the ship who kept the guns in good working order and who were in charge of firing those guns when necessary. Giving orders became second nature to him. And having those orders instantly obeyed was expected.

"I realize that it is hard for him to come back home and accept the fact that I have been an independent person while he was gone, but it is also hard for me to accept the constant censure and criticism from him. And the fact that he does not want me to go to church was the last straw. I went to Bible study on Wednesday evening and when I came home, I found him packed and ready for his father to pick him up. I yelled at him and told him to go. Let his mama treat him like a baby again and do everything for him. I have not been able to talk to him since then. He did not respond to me on Thanksgiving either," Helen explained.

"Most young men who have been injured in war and are scarred in some way are very sensitive about the way they look. It is very hard for David to accept that his body is not perfect anymore. He does not want to admit that he has any kind of imperfection and is afraid you will think less of him because of it. David will always have a limp. He is having a hard time accepting that," Dr. Walker explained.

"I told him I meant it when I said, 'for better or worse, in sickness and in health,' but he doesn't want to believe me, I guess. What can I do, Doctor?"

"I will talk to David next time I see him. I think his next appointment with me is next week. I should get an update on his therapy by then. I know that he is up on the parallel bars, walking and putting weight on the leg, so it should not be long before he is able to walk on his own. He will be using a cane for a while but will eventually be able to get rid of that too," the doctor explained to Helen. "We will discuss his future then. I know that he is due to be separated from the Navy at the first of the year. I haven't heard what his plans are after that."

"I haven't either. He hasn't talked to me about the future," Helen said sarcastically.

"Don't get too discouraged, Mrs. Cunningham. I will talk to David and see if I can get him to consider moving back home with you. He has told me a little about his mother, and it seems to me it would be difficult to live with a woman as possessive as she is," he said to Helen.

"Thank you, doctor," Helen said as she left the office.

Helen was glad she had Stanley waiting for her when she got to the car. She was still discouraged about David and did not know what was going to happen. At least she had the dog to make her smile, plus she had the responsibility of taking care of him, so she felt useful. He didn't talk back to her or criticize her every move or action.

When she got back home, she took Stanley for a short walk before going inside. The mail had come while she had been gone. She looked through the bills and advertisements, and in among the bills was a letter from David. She unlocked the door, let Stanley inside, and laid the mail down on the kitchen table. She made sure Stanley had water and food, hung her coat in the closet, and sat down at the table to read her letter.

"Dear Helen," the letter started. "I need to apologize to you for my actions. I'm not sure what I was thinking, moving in with my parents. I have treated you so horribly. I am not sure what has come over me. For all the years of the war, I have been used to taking orders and obeying them instantly, or giving orders and expecting them to be obeyed instantly. It is hard to get past that attitude of being listened to and obeyed. Most of the time there was no discussion about doing something; it was just done. I had forgotten what it was like to have a give-and-take relationship. I need to learn that all over again," David wrote. "As far as our making love, you have no idea how much I want that, but I am afraid that when you see my leg, you will be turned off and not want to touch me. I have always prided myself on being fit and strong, and now I am not. Will you continue to love me the way I am now?"

David continued to write, "You have become a strong, independent woman while I have been gone, and I don't know how to react to that. Anyway, I want to tell you that I will be separated from the Navy at the end of February, and I want to go to school and get a degree in business and accounting. I have always been good with numbers, and I think I would like to work with them somehow. I can go to school on the GI Bill and have all of my schooling paid for. I would like to attend the University of Portland. It is not far from home and is a very good school. What do you think? Could we manage with me going to school and not working for a while?"

David continued writing, "If it is okay with you, I am going to ask my dad to bring me home. My mother is in bad shape. I have suggested to Dad that she have some sort of therapy or go back to the hospital in Salem. She has been treating me like I was a baby, and sometimes I have to physically push her off of me and tell her to leave me alone. She hovers constantly. I hope you will let me in the house when Dad brings me by. I want to come home and be with you and only you. He will come to the door and ask you before I get out of the car. I love you, Helen!" David concluded and signed it only, "David."

Helen's heart was beating fast. She wondered what had happened to David at his parents' house. She had only spoken with Dr. Walker today, so he didn't have time to see or talk to

David. Apparently, his mother did not have as much influence over him as she thought she did. David seemed to be aware of the condition that his mother was in.

The idea of David going to school pleased her very much. She had wanted to finish school too, but they got married, and she never had the chance. Now he would finish, get a degree, and have it paid for under the GI Bill. Maybe Oregon State College would give him credit for the one year that he went there. He did get pretty good grades during that year, and his high school grades were very good.

Helen walked into the bedroom to make sure everything was in order. She did not know when David would come home, and she was afraid to call and ask. It was possible that Alice did not know that he was leaving, and she did not want to upset David's plans.

After making sure the bedroom was in order, the bed made and everything was in its proper place, she went and sat down on the sofa to have a talk with Stanley. She wasn't sure how he would react to David or how David would react to him.

When Helen talked to Stanley, it seemed to her that he was avidly listening to everything she said. He would cock his head a certain way as if to indicate that he understood. She loved that about him. He was such a responsive dog. Hopefully, David would love him too.

Not knowing when David would be here, Helen was afraid to leave the house. She had some grocery shopping to do, but it would have to wait. She decided to go ahead and get the Christmas decorations out and start going through them to figure out where she was going to put everything. She would have to move the furniture around a bit in the living room to be able to put the tree in front of the window, but that wouldn't be too difficult. No matter what David had said, she was going to have a Christmas tree this year. She had this lovely house, and she wanted her first Christmas in it to be perfect. And it wouldn't be without a tree.

Helen had the sofa, coffee table, and both occasional chairs covered with boxes of Christmas decorations when the doorbell rang. She had been concentrating on what she was doing and was startled when she heard the ring. She jumped up off of her knees and ran to the door, opened it up, and found David on the front porch. He had wheeled himself up the ramp and was sitting there with his suitcase in his lap. His dad had stayed in the car after retrieving the wheelchair from the trunk.

All of a sudden, Stanley appeared beside Helen with a quizzical look on his face, gave one bark, and put his paws up on David's knees.

"Well, who is this?" David asked, looking at Helen.

"This is Stanley. He has been a member of the household for a week now and has made himself very much at home. He and I had a talk this morning after I read your letter. I wanted him to understand that you would be living here too," Helen explained.

Stanley put his paws back on the porch and promptly turned around and went back inside. It seemed that he was saying to David, "Follow me, I will show you the way." Helen stepped aside so that David could wheel himself inside.

"I am sorry it is such a mess in here. I have been sorting through the Christmas decorations. I was going to go out tomorrow morning and get a tree. I know you didn't want one, but I do. I want to decorate this house with all of the decorations that we have," Helen explained.

"I think that is a great idea. May I help you pick one out?" David asked.

Helen dropped to her knees beside his chair, put her arms around his neck, and laid her head on his shoulder. "Of course, you can. I love you, and you are my husband. I want us to be partners in everything." Helen lifted her head up and gave David a quizzical look, then gave him a kiss on the lips as a welcome home.

David responded to the kiss and gave back in kind, only maybe his arms went around his wife a little tighter than they normally would have.

"I moved back into the bedroom when you left. I hope you don't mind," Helen said as she led David into the bedroom to put his things away. Stanley followed very closely, not knowing what was going to happen.

David moved from his wheelchair to the edge of the bed to take his boots off. Helen kneeled down between his legs and gave him another kiss, gradually taking his jacket, then his shirt off. She continued to unbuckle his belt and open his zipper on his trousers. "Are you sure, Helen?" David asked.

"I wouldn't be here if I wasn't sure. It has been much too long since we have made love to each other. David was able to stand up beside the bed, using it for support while he took his trousers off and helped Helen remove her clothes, all the time kissing her on the face, neck, and lips.

As both of them climbed into bed, Helen noticed that David's bad leg was on the other side of her, and he covered it with the sheet right away.

"It's okay, David. I love you as you are, bad leg and all. It does not repulse me or make me afraid. Just make love to me," she begged.

And they did just that, with Stanley laying on his rug beside the bed.

They made love to each other several times that night, and both of them finally fell into a deep sleep, and it was 8:30 AM when they awoke the next morning. Helen helped David take a shower, and while he was dressing, she took Stanley out for a much-needed walk. He was a very good dog for not disturbing them all night. He seemed to know that they needed this time together.

When Helen and Stanley returned to the house, David had coffee ready and decided he needed to get acquainted with Stanley while Helen fixed them some breakfast.

"Honey, this dog is fantastic. Where did you get him?" David asked.

"I found him at the humane society," Helen explained and proceeded to tell him about how she and Stanley met. "I just knew he was my dog. I have arranged for someone to come this week and fence the backyard. I thought it would be a good idea to do the whole yard. It will cost us about $75.00, but I think it is worth it. Dad made Stanley a great dog house. It even has his name over the door, but I can't leave him outside yet with no fence."

"In the spring, we can have a garden since the yard will be fenced. We might have to fence just the garden area to keep this guy here out of it," David said as he looked at Stanley.

While they were eating their breakfast, Helen asked David, "What happened with your mother?"

"You were certainly right about her odd behavior. It was like she wanted me to be her little baby again. She certainly treated me like one. When I would sit on the sofa, she would sit as close as she could to me, put her arms around me, and want to cradle me like a baby. Helen, she even wanted to give me a bath!" David said incredulously.

"What did your dad do when she was doing this?" Helen asked.

"There wasn't much he could do. She shooed him away most of the time. I finally told her to lay off. I was a big boy now and could take care of myself, but she really didn't listen. She would hear only what she wanted to hear," David said. "Dad and I talked, and he has admitted that he is going to have to commit her to the hospital in Salem again. She will really flip out now with me gone. Expect either phone calls or a visit from her."

"Did she say bad things about me?" Helen asked meekly.

"She tried to, but I wouldn't listen to her," David answered.

Life was good again for David and Helen. They got their Christmas tree, decorated it, and were very happy with the results. David contacted Oregon State College and was able to get his transcript from when he was a student there. He registered for classes at the University of Portland for the winter term to start in January. They accepted the credits he had received at Oregon State, so he was able to register as a sophomore.

Helen finally told David about the possibility of a job at Sears as an inventory control clerk. He was hesitant at first, but then thought, with him in school, it would be good for Helen to have a job to keep her busy. He realized that it was basically the same job she did for four years at Continental Can Co.

Mr. Jacobs, the personnel manager at Sears, finally called Helen on Friday, November 30, and offered her the job as inventory clerk. She would start work on Monday, December 3rd.

David was able to drive the car now. His leg was strong enough to be able to move it quickly from the accelerator to the brake while using the clutch with his other foot. It was decided that David would take Helen to work when he could, but she was able to take the bus if he wasn't available. The bus stopped right in front of the store. David would use the car to go back and forth to school as his class schedule would probably be different every day.

The yard had been fenced, and Stanley was able to spend some time outside without David or Helen having to be with him. David thought that it might be a good idea to put a dog door in the back door so that Stanley could come in and out as he pleased. He called Willard, and together they were able to install it themselves. Stanley was now able to come and go as he pleased, and he loved it. For a couple of days, he kept going in and out, but he soon got used to the fact that he wasn't going to be shut out.

Chapter 21

◆ ◆ ◆ ◆ ◆

*H*elen found her job fascinating. She worked closely with the department managers and assistant managers.

It did not take her long to understand the system of inventory control that the store used. Once a year, in January, they closed the store for one day and did a complete, thorough inventory of all of the merchandise in the store. Then, every month, the managers would report the current inventory to her department. This monthly inventory was used for reordering purposes. The annual inventory was for tax purposes. The store had to report the value of their inventory to headquarters in Chicago so that the company could report it on their tax forms. It was a massive job to have every store in the country report their inventory. Helen was glad she didn't have that job.

The experience that Helen gained working at Continental Can was invaluable to her at Sears. She understood the need to get the figures correct, not only for tax purposes but mainly for reordering the merchandise. She would report the figures to the merchandise managers, and their job, with the help of the department managers, was to figure out what was selling well and had to be reordered or what was not selling and could be suspended to make room for something new. The store was always adding merchandise lines and was always aware of what was popular and what was not.

Helen enjoyed the companionship of the other women also. There was a large lunchroom where she took her coffee break twice a day, and she would sit and chat with some of the other women who worked in the store. Several of the girls mentioned that they were going through some rough times adjusting to their husbands being back home and had taken the job at Sears to build some self-confidence and to feel good about themselves again. Helen was very quiet about her situation with David and never mentioned any of their problems to the other ladies. She was just very thankful that David was willing to work on their differences and try to solve them.

"Did you have problems when your husband came home?" one of the girls asked Helen one day.

"I am sure everyone had some problems. We were without them for four years, and it is hard to relinquish some of the control that we had during that time. But I think that if everyone is willing to talk to and listen to each other, things will work out. I have learned over the years that one has to compromise and be willing to give up a little to receive a lot," Helen answered, without revealing any of the difficulties that she and David had.

With the help of Rev. Corbin, they had learned to talk over a problem as it occurs and not let it fester for any time. He suggested that if the argument was getting out of hand, to sit and cool off a bit, then begin to discuss solutions. Rev. Corbin also said that they should never go to bed angry with each other. And they should always say, "I love you!" before they go to sleep. Since David and Helen had started doing that, their relationship was getting better all of the time.

Christmas was a happy time for them this year. Their house was decorated inside with all of the beautiful things that they had accumulated. The Christmas tree was placed in front of the large living room window. Helen meticulously put the tinsel on the tree, one strand at a time. She could remember her mother putting it on so carefully each year, only to have her brother Richard come along and grab a bunch and just throw it at the tree. His mother would get so mad at Richard but would laugh at him at the same time. Christmas was always a happy time in the Martin household, and David and Helen were determined to keep it that way in their home.

On Christmas morning, Willard and Jane went to Helen and David's house for Christmas breakfast and to open presents. Gloria and Marian and their families had gone to their respective in-laws for the morning gift opening. They would meet later in the day at Willard and Jane's for their Christmas dinner.

Just before they were ready to open their gifts, the doorbell rang. Helen was startled but got up to answer it. Who would come visiting on Christmas morning? she wondered.

There, sitting in front of the door, was a brand-new washing machine. Helen screamed, turned, looked at David, and started to cry. It seems that Willard and David had arranged for a couple of Willard's friends to deliver it that morning. They were both standing out of sight of the front door. After Helen got over the shock, Willard invited them in, and they helped to get the washer to the basement and hooked up.

Helen could not believe that David had done that for her.

"You need a washer, honey. You can't be hauling our dirty clothes to your parents every week. Anyway, I was able to use your employee discount. I will be paying it off in four weeks, so we won't have a lot of interest to pay," he explained.

"You know, before I got this job, I was thinking that if I did get it, I could use the discount and purchase a washing machine. That was before you came home, and I wasn't sure about the future in this house. Thank you so much, David," Helen said again.

She felt a little funny about the gifts she had gotten for David now. She had bought him a new bathrobe. His old one was threadbare and needed to be cut up into rags. She also got him some new slacks and shirts for school. A lot of his civilian clothes were too small for him. He had filled out while he was in the Navy, and his shirts would not button.

Helen started to apologize for what she had bought for him compared to her gift from him, but David said, "No! This is exactly what I need. I have had that bathrobe since I was in high school, and I desperately need clothes for school. I can't wear my uniform after next month, and I didn't have anything decent to wear. I love all of it."

David was able to walk with a cane now and was relieved to not have to rely on the wheelchair. He would be able to navigate the halls of the university without having to worry about stairs.

School was due to start on the 17th of January. David had gone through all of the orientation, was able to take all of the classes that he signed up for, and knew where every class was located on campus. Because he was taking business and accounting classes, most of them were in the same general area. He had a Humanities class he had to take in order to graduate, but right now that was the only required class he was lacking. All of the classes he took at Oregon State would transfer over and meet his graduation requirements for the University of Portland.

David had met several of the men who were in his business classes at orientation. They were also going to school courtesy of the GI Bill. A couple of the men were in Europe during the war, but most of them were in the Pacific. Some were Marines and the others were Sailors. David had heard from their conversations with each other that they were also having trouble adjusting to civilian life. Coming home to wives who were independent women was the hardest. When they left in 1941, their wives and children were totally dependent on them. Now, the children turned to their mothers for advice and guidance, and many of them didn't know their fathers. They were too young when the war started and their fathers left.

From their talk, none of them indicated that they had any idea what their wives went through while they were gone. David hadn't at first. The idea that Helen had to learn a whole new way of life in a very short time was totally foreign to him. He thought that he was the only one having to make changes when he left and the only one making the changes when he returned.

David spoke up while the men were talking and said, "You know, it almost cost me my marriage because I was too thickheaded to understand what my wife went through when I left."

"What do you mean, what your wife went through? She got to stay in her nice warm home without the drastic changes to her life that we had to endure. The wives had it easy," the man said to David.

"Think about it! All of a sudden, her support was gone. If you had children, she had 100 percent responsibility for them. How many times had your wife changed a tire? Had she ever paid a bill before or even written a check or balanced the checkbook? Had she ever had to deal with a power outage by herself? Did she know how to turn the power off or on or even know where the fuse box was in your house? Had she ever mowed the lawn, replaced a broken window? Was she ever scared when there was a noise outside and you were not around to check it out? Think about it. Not only your life turned upside down, but so did hers. And many times, she went to work doing work in factories, shipyards, and plants to keep the country and the war going. That was totally foreign to her. And by God, she did a fantastic job of keeping everything going. Fellows, please don't put your wives down. They are angels here on earth!" David expounded.

David turned to leave the table, thinking that the men would not want to talk to him anymore. He was afraid he had made some enemies, but in unison, the men clapped and said thank you.

"You gave us a lot to think about. Thank you. How did you come about all this knowledge you seem to have?" another man asked him.

"By trial and lots of error. I almost lost her because I was too pig-headed and stupid to realize what I had and how much I needed her in my life. We don't have any kids yet, but I pray to God every day that when we do, they are just like her," David said as he started to walk away. "I have to get home. I am taking my wife out to dinner this evening, and I don't want to be late."

"You are one lucky guy!" another one said.

"I know!" David answered as he waved goodbye.

David was attending church with Helen on Sunday mornings. He found the service so calming and comfortable. The entire congregation welcomed him like he was one of them already. Reverend Corbin was not a Bible-thumping type of preacher. His messages were down to earth and easily understood and adaptable to everyday life.

They were on their way over to Helen's parents' home for dinner after church. David had not had a family dinner with everyone there since he had been home. He had been avoiding all of Helen's relatives.

David was greeted warmly by Willard and Jane and ushered into the living room. Josh, Gloria's husband, said, "Well, you finally decided to grace us with your presence, huh! Did you think you were too good for the likes of us?" Everyone in the room was shocked at what he had said.

"Josh, that was really uncalled for," Willard said. "David has not been well and until a couple of weeks ago was in a wheelchair. He was not able to move the chair around in our house very easily."

"Thank you, Willard. No, Josh, that was not it at all. I was ill and didn't feel that I was able to cope with being around a crowd of people, even family. I am feeling much better now and am better able to deal with people," David answered politely. Gloria and Marian greeted him with handshakes and friendly greetings, but no hugs like there used to be. He guessed that they resented him for what he had done to their sister or that their husbands wouldn't allow them to hug another man, even if it was their brother-in-law.

When they sat down to dinner, David noticed that the little girls were very quiet and hardly spoke at all. When he asked them about school, they only had one or two-word answers to the questions. He also noticed that both Josh and Michael's eyes were on them most of the time and that they were constantly harping at them. It was either sit up straight, stop slurping your soup, take smaller bites, clean your plate, etc. The little girls were always so verbal and outgoing, and now they were like little mice, just sitting, waiting to be pounced on. David was really sorry to see the girls in the state they were in. It appeared they were scared to death of their dads.

David really wanted to talk to his brothers-in-law and tell them basically the same thing he had said to the students at school, but both Josh and Michael were totally unreceptive to what David had to say. He started the conversation a couple of times, but their response was to butt out, that he didn't have kids and didn't know what he was talking about.

When David and Helen were driving home, David asked about Josh and Michael.

"Both Gloria and Marian are at their wit's end," Helen said. "They do not know what to do. The guys treat them the same way they do the girls. Gloria said that Josh constantly criticizes her for almost everything she does. He is dissatisfied with almost every meal she cooks, even down to complaining about the coffee in the morning. Josh even objects to her wardrobe. It's funny because it is the same wardrobe she had before Josh left. She has not spent any money on clothes for herself in four years. She only bought one new pair of shoes in all that time. Mom and Dad bought both she and Marian some things for their birthdays and for Christmas, but every penny spent for clothing went to the girls. They were outgrowing all of their clothes and had to have new ones. Even at that, the things that were purchased were the least expensive they could find," Helen continued. "It hurts my heart to hear Josh and Michael talk to them the way they do. But there is not really much I can say or do. I want to be there to support my sisters and do not want to alienate either Josh or Michael, let alone get caught up in their domestic problems."

"That's probably best for now. We are working on our own issues and don't need to get involved in anyone else's, and I certainly do not feel comfortable giving advice," David added.

Chapter 22

ife became a pleasant routine for David and Helen. Helen worked from 8:30 AM to 5:00 PM, five days a week. She had Saturday and Sunday off. David went to school four days a week, Tuesday through Friday, with Monday as a study day. On Monday evenings, he joined the men's Bible study class at church. He had never read any of the Bible before and was totally new to all of the studies, but all of the men were very accommodating and helped him to understand the lessons and what the meaning of the verses were. David found it fascinating and loved going to the classes. He would usually pick Helen up at work on Mondays, drop her off at home, and head to church.

She continued with her Bible study group on Wednesdays with the added benefit of graduating to making neck scarves for the needy.

Neither Helen nor David had been baptized. As Easter approached, both of them decided that they would like to be baptized before Easter Sunday. Rev. Corbin met with them on Sunday afternoons to give them some instruction in the church, and on Sunday, April 7th, they were both baptized. It was a lovely ceremony with a reception afterward in the social hall. Willard and Jane Martin came, and David's dad was invited but declined, saying that Sunday was his day to visit Alice at the hospital in Salem. Unfortunately, Roger reported that Alice was not getting any better and would be staying in the hospital indefinitely. He told David that there were times when she didn't even know him.

School was going very well for David. He was getting top grades in all of his classes and enjoying each of them very much. He felt very positive about his future.

In late May, Helen felt that she was coming down with the flu. She felt terrible with an upset stomach for days on end. She went to work every day but felt sluggish and out of sorts most of the time. She was beginning to snap at David over the silliest things, and she was in tears a lot of the time over nothing at all.

David thought he knew what was wrong but was afraid to mention it to her. He had noticed that she had not had a monthly cycle for a couple of months, and he thought she was probably pregnant.

"Helen, this has been going on long enough. Call in sick on Monday, and I am taking you to the doctor. I am tired of you being sick all of the time."

"I don't have time to miss work. There is too much to do. I will be fine. It will go away pretty soon," Helen announced.

"If you don't call, I will. I am worried about you, honey, and I want you to see the doctor," he begged her.

"Oh, all right. I'll go," she conceded.

After Helen dressed, she walked into the doctor's private office and found David sitting there. She was surprised to see him there and became instantly afraid that something serious was wrong with her.

"What is wrong with me, Doctor?" Helen asked with a scared look on her face.

"Nothing that another six months won't cure," he told her.

David had a great big smile on his face, and Helen looked at him like he was crazy. She still didn't understand.

"We are going to have a baby, sweetheart. You are three months pregnant," David said as he reached over and took her hand in his.

"I can't be pregnant. I have too much to do at work. How am I going to have a baby and work too?" she asked. She was stunned at the news. It was the last thing that she had thought of. She had not realized that she had missed her cycle. She was busy and didn't even think of it.

"I think your baby is going to make an appearance sometime in the latter part of December," the doctor told them. "Helen, I want you to take these vitamins daily, get plenty of exercise, and plenty of rest. Try not to lift anything very heavy and put your feet up as often as you can. You will start feeling better in a couple of weeks. Usually, this yucky feeling goes away about the fourth month of pregnancy. Do you have any questions?"

"Yes," said Helen. "How could this happen? I was so good about using the diaphragm."

"Nothing is 100 percent guaranteed to work. Sometimes it is just your time to have a baby. Now seems to be your time. I want to see you back in here in a month," he said to both of them.

Helen was very quiet on the way home from the doctor's office.

"We will figure it out, sweetheart," David said to her. "You are young and healthy and right now, I think, the most beautiful woman in the world."

Helen took his hand for a moment and squeezed it. She was totally overwhelmed and couldn't say anything. She had wanted children right after she was married, but she and David had decided to wait a couple of years to get on their feet and have some money set aside for a better home. Their little apartment was too small for a baby. Then the war came along and put a hold on all family plans.

Helen saw her sisters with their children and the way they had to cope with little ones during the war, and she was glad that they had waited. When David first got home, she would not have wanted to get pregnant at all. Their life together was too uncertain. Now, she was working full-time at a good job and making some decent money, and David was in school fulltime. How are they going to find the time to have a baby?

"I am going to lay down for a bit," Helen said when they got home from the doctor's office. "I am tired and need to absorb all of this news."

"You go rest, honey. I will heat up some leftover vegetable soup for us for lunch when you are ready," David told her.

"Thanks," she said as she headed for the bedroom.

About an hour later, David gently opened the bedroom door to check on his wife and found her curled into a ball on the bed, crying her eyes out. He walked over to the bed, laid down beside her, and took her into his arms.

"Honey, it will be alright. We will figure things out. I love you so much, and I love our baby inside of you," David said as he held her close.

"I know we will work things out, and we will love this baby so much. It is just such a shock. We have been married for almost eight years, and we are just starting our family. Most people that have been married as long as we have kids in school by now," Helen said.

"I know, but just think how much better off we will be. We are older and wiser and have a more settled life. Any hitches that come along, we will take care of," David announced. "Are you hungry? I'm starved! Let's eat some soup. Hopefully, that will stay down for you. I would hate it if the baby did not like your vegetable soup. It is one of my favorites," David said as he was helping Helen up from bed.

Helen laughed, got up, and went into the bathroom to wash her face while David went to serve up the very good vegetable soup.

After telling Willard and Jane Martin the news, David went to visit his father to let him know. Helen didn't offer to go with him. She was still afraid of some backlash from Roger. He was so torn up about his wife that she was not sure of his reactions and wanted to avoid any conflict.

"Dad, you need to get someone in to clean this house. It is a mess," David said after he greeted his father.

"I know. Alice would be horrified if she saw it, but I just don't have the heart or the energy to get someone in here. I really need to pick things up and put them away, but again, I don't have the energy," Roger explained. "What brings you here today?"

"Helen and I have some news," David started to say before Roger interrupted him.

"Are you leaving her? That would make Alice so happy. Maybe she would get well enough to come home then," Roger asked with a hopeful look on his face.

"Of course not, Dad! I am not going to leave Helen, so get that idea out of your head. Mom will just have to get used to the fact that I am married to Helen, and it is going to stay that way. No, I came over here to tell you that we are having a baby. It is due sometime in the latter part of December," David explained to his father.

"Oh! I'm not sure whether I will tell Alice that news or not. She always asks about you, but I never have much to tell her. Mostly she just sits and stares out the window. I read to her a lot, but I am not sure if she hears me or not. She is in her own world," Roger told him.

"We are very excited about the baby, Dad. We had hoped that you would be excited too. I wish you would come over for dinner some evening. You know, Helen is a very good cook," David asked.

"I remember, but I just can't come over as long as Alice objects to her so much. It would not be fair to my wife," Roger answered.

"What does the doctor say about Mom?" David inquired.

"Not much. She is in good health physically, except that she needs to eat more and exercise more, but her mind is going very quickly. You know, David, sometimes I don't think that Alice will ever come home," Roger said with tears in his eyes.

"I'm sorry, Dad. I wish I could do something to help, but at this point, she would not listen to me, and I will not leave Helen for her," David said to his dad as he gave him a hug. "I just came by to let you know we were having a baby. I thought you would be happy to hear that you will be a grandfather. I am truly sorry for Mom, but as I said, there is nothing I can do now," David continued.

"I know, and thanks for coming by. I appreciate the visit, and congratulations on the news. I am happy for you," Roger related as David was getting ready to leave.

"And Dad, please get someone in to clean this place up. It really smells bad, and you shouldn't be living this way. You are always invited to come have a meal with us also. Don't forget that," David told his dad as he walked out the door.

He felt bad about his dad, and he loved both of his parents, but right now he couldn't become involved in their dramatic life. His mom would probably never come home, and unless his dad accepted that and started acting like he cared, David couldn't become involved.

When he told Helen about the visit with his dad, she agreed that they couldn't become immersed in the Cunninghams' problems. They had to figure out their own lives right now, and they had enough going on without taking on any more. She was really sorry for both Roger and Alice, but couldn't and wouldn't become involved.

Life became a pleasant routine for both David and Helen. They didn't tell anyone else about the pregnancy yet, not even Helen's sisters. They were so busy with their own lives right now. Neither of them was very happy in their marriages. Their husbands were giving them a hard time about almost everything they did. They couldn't cook a decent meal, they didn't clean the house properly, they didn't iron their shirts the right way, and the worst complaint was that they weren't doing a good job of raising their girls. All four of Helen's nieces' grades had gone down since their dads had come home from the war, and they were not getting any better with the men taking over their regimen and disciplining. Their whole personalities had changed, and it broke Helen's heart.

Helen was afraid to tell them that she was having a baby. She didn't know what Josh and Michael would say to her or to David, and she did not want to have any more conflict in the family than there already was. Every time they got together for a family dinner, some derogatory comment was made about Helen and David. They wanted to avoid any more comments. She would wait until she began to show before she said anything.

Helen found out that she could take a three-month maternity leave of absence at Sears. She would be able to stay home with the baby for three months and then go back to work. She would be guaranteed the same job when she returned. Jane had offered to watch her grandchild while Helen worked and while David was in school. He would take care of the baby when he was home. It would interfere with his study schedule, but that was to be expected. He was going to be a hands-on father. He firmly believed that it was not just the mother's job to care for the children. He would take an active role in the care of their child.

They talked a lot about the baby, whether it would be a boy or a girl. Helen wanted a son who looked just like David, and David wanted a daughter who looked just like Helen. They both laughed a lot and were supremely happy with life. Helen was beginning to show a little, and she finally decided to privately tell her sisters. They were both very happy for her and offered maternity clothes and baby clothes when the time came.

The spare bedroom would be turned into a nursery. Marion still had the crib that her twins used and offered it to Helen. They would have to get a few items of furniture, but with both sisters offering her their extra things, they wouldn't need much. Apparently, the brothers-in-law had no objections to getting the stuff out of their houses.

It was a hot summer in Portland in 1946, and Helen was miserable a lot of the time. She was very glad she would be in her last three months of pregnancy during the cooler months of fall. She couldn't imagine being hugely pregnant in the very hot summer months.

David went to school during the summer months so that he would be that much ahead and be able to get his degree that much sooner. He had been looking at possible part-time jobs where he could use his accounting knowledge in a practical way, but so far, he hadn't found anything on a part-time basis. He was hopeful, though.

Helen finally had to quit work just before Thanksgiving. Her doctor wanted her to get more rest and to have her feet up at least four hours a day. She couldn't do that at work.

Some of the ladies at work gave her a baby shower. She received some lovely things and was very grateful for all of it. The very practical things like diapers, blankets, and sleepers were the most appreciated, but she also was thrilled with all of the handmade items that she received. All of the ladies at her Bible study class either knitted or crocheted sweaters, hats, or blankets for the baby.

Along with what her sisters had given to her, her baby would be very well dressed. It would probably outgrow a lot of the clothes before it got to wear them.

On Saturday, December 7th, David went to a ceremony at the VFW hall to commemorate the bombing of Pearl Harbor. There was a lot of news about the fifth anniversary of the bombing. Helen stayed home. She was too uncomfortable to battle the crowds.

Ten days later, on the 17th, Helen was standing at the kitchen sink washing up some breakfast dishes when she felt a very sharp pain in her stomach. She was startled and cried out. David came running and found her doubled over in extreme pain. He called the doctor, who told him to get her to Emanuel Hospital as soon as possible, and he would meet them there. David went to the bedroom, picked up Helen's suitcase, which had been packed for over a week, and led her to the car. All of the time, she was moaning in pain.

The doctor met them at the hospital, and about seven hours later, Helen gave birth to a beautiful baby boy. He weighed in at 7 lbs. 12 oz. and was 19 inches long, and they named him Robert David Cunningham.

On December 24th, David took his wife and son home from the hospital to a house filled with Christmas decorations and a tree piled with presents. But the best thing of all was that Stanley was sitting in the hallway waiting for his family to come home.

He had a huge dog smile on his face to greet his new playmate.